The Immeasurable Man
(It's been real.)

Wes Payton

Published by Rogue Phoenix Press, LLP
Copyright © 2024

ISBN: 978-1-62420-811-9

Credits
Editor: Christie L. Kraemer
Cover: Designs by Ms G

Dedication

For Alan Van Natter, a man who possessed an immeasurable spirit.

Prologue

Future generations will never believe the ingenuousness of the people I'm going to tell you about—it would strain credulity, as they say...so, for posterity's sake, let's call all of what comes next a work of fiction.

I exist in extreme isolation. I've been immunocompromised since birth, and though now in my mid-thirties, I have no memory of ever having had direct human contact. Until recently, all my knowledge of human interaction was theoretical; however, since the side effects of my sequestration were identified a couple of years back, my aptitudes have become very much in demand.

Aptitude One: Decisiveness. I don't hesitate when making decisions, and I don't second guess myself—ever. Why should I? My formative years were spent almost exclusively in study. I've seen every film worth seeing since the dawn of cinema. You learned how to be human from your fallible family, your fatuous friends, and your chucklehead classmates. I learned courage from Errol Flynn, self-confidence from Clark Gable, forbearance from Humphrey Bogart, resolve from Sidney Poitier, humor from Groucho Marx, and how to see right through someone from Bette Davis.

Aptitude Two: Detachment. Given my circumstances, this one hardly requires explanation, except to say that while being detached may not seem like an aptitude, in my case it is...or rather, it is in the cases I'm assigned. I literally have no skin in the game—my impartiality has never been questioned, rendering my decisions unassailable, which in this litigious age is advantageous to say the least. You can't sue a ghost...you'll see what I mean in a moment.

Aptitude Three: Discernment. I don't claim—though others have—to possess a particularly great mind, but I doubt you'll ever encounter a less cluttered mind than mine. Everything I know, everything I've experienced has come to me through the portal that is my domicile's viewscreen, all of which I've fastidiously categorized and catalogued. I have access—just like you—to nearly unlimited knowledge, but unlike you that flow of information isn't impeded by off-screen obligations and outside influences or encumbered by eventual disinterest. I simply have nothing else to do. My high-definition conduit to the world is all I have, and through it I have observed all.

So those are the 3 Ds of me, though I doubt my brief description has left you with a sketch that's very three dimensional—gramercy Groucho! If you'd like to understand my situation better, I invite you to spend a few days with me...everything really got started on what I'd been led to believe was the second Tuesday of February.

Act I

Chapter One

Arlo sat uncomfortably on the couch in the bank's waiting area, reading a months-old copy of Architectural Digest. His suit didn't fit well, his beard itched, his stomach was doing somersaults, his hearing aid—which he usually barely noticed—felt like it might fall out of his ear at any moment, and the pistol tucked into his waistband poked against the vertebrae in the small of his back. He thought he might've disengaged its safety when he'd sat down. Also, he had no idea what a flying buttress was despite having just perused an article about their modern usage, and he had to pee.

He furtively glanced over at his brother, Dylan, who stood near a small table lined with short stacks of deposit slips. He looked more like a loiterer than a customer. His fulsome beard and sweating brow gave him the appearance of someone who only stopped in for the free air conditioning. Dylan nodded, and Arlo turned to see the bank manager approaching.

"Good morning," signed the bank manager (translated from ASL).

Arlo stood, hoping his gun wouldn't slide down the back of his trousers. "I'm so pleased someone here knows sign language. I wear a hearing aid, but really it only allows me to hear car horns and alarms." He quickly dropped his hands, wishing he hadn't mentioned alarms.

"My daughter was born deaf, so whenever a customer comes in who signs, my employees let me know—frankly, I prefer signing to talking...the conversations tend to be less discursive."

Arlo smiled. "I quite agree...besides, so many people have unattractive faces, but ugly hands are a rarity."

The manager chuckled. "That's a good point. Follow me to my office, and we'll discuss how I can help you today."

The two walked in step along the tile floor dividing the tellers' counters from the loan officers' cubicles to the lone, walled office at the back of the bank. The manager opened the door for Arlo to enter and motioned to a wingback chair facing a double pedestal desk. Then he shut the door and sat in his desk chair. "I noticed that you were reading an architecture magazine. You may be interested to know that this bank is a converted bus station...what once was a depot is now a place to make a deposit."

"Then where does one go to catch a bus around here?" Arlo asked with gesticulating hands.

"I don't know...perhaps Greyhound has designs to convert the old Wells Fargo building three blocks over." The manger studied Arlo's face for a moment. "Have we met before?"

"I don't think so...this is my first time coming here."

"No, I know I haven't seen you in here before, but you remind me of someone I was introduced to at a benefit that I attended with my daughter a few months back—an inquisitive young man, though now I recall him being somewhat younger than you...or at least cleanshaven."

Arlo shook his head. "I'm new in town, so I'm sure it wasn't me that you're remembering."

The manager nodded. "Probably not then...so I understand you want to make a deposit with us today."

"No, a withdrawal," Arlo signed emphatically.

"Oh, I was told by the teller you communicated with that you were dropping off, not picking up. I'll access your account." The manager tapped at the keyboard on his desk. "Do you have an ID? I assume your account was set up at one of our other branches since you're new to the area."

"A sizeable withdrawal," signed Arlo insistently.

"Yes, I understand."

"I don't think you do." Arlo held up an index finger to signal for a pause as he pulled the pistol from under his jacket.

~ * ~

IM paused the viewscreen as his domicile's speaker chimed. "Hello there."

"IM, are you available for an assignment?"

"I can never tell if you're being sarcastic or courteous when you ask me that."

"Usually a bit of both."

"I didn't think that was possible," replied IM.

"Maybe it isn't, but your skill set is needed right now to address a relatively isolated situation that could escalate into a national headline if not dealt with promptly, so let's call it the latter and move on, shall we?"

"By all means."

"Good then, an attempted heist of a financial services institution located in the U.S. state of—"

"A bank robbery—isn't that a bit...mundane for me?"

"It's developed into a hostage situation."

"The local constabulary doesn't have a negotiator on staff?" asked IM.

"Your services were specifically requested by the well-connected father of one of the bank customers who's currently being held hostage."

"Okay, send me the details."

"I'm IM'ing you them now, IM."

IM studied the data on his viewscreen for a moment. "Ah, something of a quandary I see."

"It would seem the strategy of the four bearded bandits was to have two of them take over the bank manager's office, the only enclosed room in the otherwise open-floorplan building, which also happens not to be equipped with a surveillance camera, while the other two guarded the front door. Apparently, the two in the office convinced the manager to instruct his employees to gather up all the cash they could and stack it outside his office door. However, soon after they did so, the lobby cameras caught all six employees and ten customers flinching simultaneously—"

"Presumably startled by a gunshot they heard from the office," interrupted IM, "so I take it there's no audio to accompany the video files I'm seeing now."

"I'm afraid not. Why do you think they would've shot the manager after he complied with having all that money piled up?"

"Possibly because he wasn't willing to comply with their next demand."

"Which was?"

"Telling his employees to round up the customers and send them into his office," answered IM, "where I suspect the robbers intended to shave their beards and mix in with the customers when they're to be set free, mistakenly believing that their gambit could defeat the facial recognition program the authorities will undoubtedly use in an attempt to track them as they make good their escape."

"That's pretty clever...you don't think shaving their beards could fool the program?"

"Even if it could, the authorities already have all the shaven customers on video, so it would only be a matter of identifying whose faces exited that weren't captured on camera entering...besides, unless the would-be robbers intend to eat their own whiskers, they'll all either leave behind a massive pile of DNA evidence or each will make their exit with a rather incriminating clue somewhere on his person—so not clever...though I suppose it's easy enough for a strong premise to outshine the weaker points of a plot. For instance, take the movie Casablanca—"

"I did mention this is a matter of some urgency, didn't I?"

"Of course," IM replied, "let's press on."

"FYI, if the assailants are convicted of murder during the commission of an armed robbery in that state, it's a mandatory life sentence."

IM shook his head. "Which means, legally speaking, they'd be in no worse circumstances if they just started killing the hostages who've seen them and then effected their escape during the ensuing pandemonium."

"As you say...a quandary."

Something on IM's screen caught his attention. "I'm reviewing the video from the lobby before the robbery began...one assailant seems to be conversing in sign language with the bank manager."

"Is that relevant?"

"It might explain how he gained access to the manager's office without putting anyone on alert...and it gives me an idea."

"Speaking of the manager's office, I was just informed that the smoke detector in there was triggered...more gunfire perhaps?"

IM scanned the live feed on his screen. "No, I'm reading concern on the faces of the customers, not startlement like before. I think the perpetrators are burning their beard trimmings...perhaps they're cleverer than I first thought."

"If they're torching evidence, then it probably means they're about to make their move."

"I agree. Link me up to a holo-case onsite and tell the authorities to toss it through the front window of the bank, but first have them freight the case with an obstreperous item I'm sending you the specs for...or something comparable, if they don't have that particular payload on hand."

~ * ~

"There's a cop coming," shouted a bewhiskered robber by the bank's inner vestibule door. "What should I do?"

"It's just one cop?" asked another hirsute gunman keeping watch over the customers and employees lying face down in the lobby.

"Looks like it...all the rest of them are still hunkered down behind their squad cars. Should I let him in?"

"Are you nuts...tell him to piss off."

"He's carrying a case."

The gunman turned toward his partner at the front door. "What's in it?"

"Sure, let me use my x-ray vision to find out."

"I mean is it big, like a footlocker, or small, like a cigar case?"

"It's just a regular briefcase sized case...seems kinda high-tech though."

"It could be full of explosives."

"Why would the cops give us explosives?" asked the robber manning the door.

"No, I mean to blow us up."

"And kill our hostages?"

"Then maybe it's full of money."

"We just robbed a bank...we don't need money—we need a way out of here."

"As if I didn't know that." The gunman turned back to the hostages on the floor. "Wait to see what he does with it."

"He...he just dropped it off outside the front door and kept on walking."

"He didn't run?"

"No...set it down like he was delivering the mail."

"If he didn't run, then it's probably not a bomb."

The robber entered the vestibule and inspected the case through the glass door. "I think it's a holo-case."

"How can you tell there's nothing in it?"

"No, not hollow...I mean it looks like it's set up to project a holographic image."

Suddenly a life-size version of IM appeared in blue light atop the case. "May I come in?"

The robber jumped back from the door. "Oh shit, it's the Immeasurable Man."

"Here?" asked the other gunman incredulously. "Aren't we...a little beneath his notice?"

"Apparently not—he's looking right at me."

"I can hear you through the case's microphone and have access to the bank's surveillance video feed," replied IM, "but my holographic image is not 'looking' at you. In fact, I only know I'm facing you because I can see my image from the camera mounted in the vestibule's ATM."

The robber turned to the ATM on the wall next to him and then back to IM, who waved to himself. "What do you want?"

"To come inside and talk calmly with you all in hopes of figuring out a way to peacefully resolve the current situation. I promise, my incorporeal form won't attempt to overpower you...that was a joke."

The robber turned back toward the gunman in the lobby. "What do you think?"

"If they sent the Immeasurable Man to negotiate with us, then there must be something in here that they want. I say we hear him out...see if we can finagle a get out of jail free card."

"Yeah...okay." The robber unlocked the padlock holding the chain tight around the handles of the outer doors of the vestibule, opened one door slightly, reached an arm out to grab the case, and then relocked the chain. "I'll take the case back to the office while you keep an eye on the hostages and the front door."

As the robber walked along the tile, carrying the case down at his side, IM's holographic figure levitated horizontally above the heads of the prone hostages. Several of them raised their heads off the floor to look at IM. "Stay calm...I'm here to help you...this ordeal will soon be over."

The robber opened the door to the manager's office and entered.

"What the hell?" gasped the manager, looking up from the carpeted floor.

IM muted his channel to the case and addressed the others on the party line. "The manager is alive. Repeat, the voice you just heard matches the vocal recognition the bank's security system has on file. The body growing colder in the corner of the room that my case's thermal sensor is picking up must be that of one of the robbers, as they're the only other two to have been captured on camera entering the office." IM unmuted the case's channel. "So to whom do I have the pleasure of speaking?"

The robber set the case on the manager's desk. "Sure, do you want our social security numbers too?"

"Point well taken. I was only attempting to be polite, but names aren't important now."

The bank manager raised his head again. "I didn't think you'd be so tall."

"Shut up and put your head back down or I'll blow it off," ordered the robber who'd brought IM into the office.

"If it would put any of you more at ease, you're welcome to adjust my height with the knob on the side of the case," said IM.

"I set you up on a desk—that's why you look so tall." The robber took off his suit jacket to reveal a basketball jersey underneath. He positioned the jacket around the case to cover its sides and most of the top, except for the lens that projected the hologram. "I believe that you can't see us, but I'm doing this in case your case has any little peephole cameras the cops stuck on it."

"Doing what?" asked IM.

The gunman tasked with keeping an eye on the hostages appeared in the office doorway. "What's going on?"

"I thought you were watching the front door."

"I can see it and all the hostages just fine from here." The gunman looked at the half-shaven and fully dead robber slumped in the corner. "Jesus, Dylan's seen better days."

IM muted his channel to the case once more. "I assume you all heard that and are now searching your criminal databases for a 'Dylan.'" He studied his screen for a moment. "I see the details coming through for a felon with a matching modus operandi who has a deaf brother named Arlo." He unmuted his case channel. "Is one of your colleagues in need of medical attention?"

"He's past that now," replied the robber who'd brought him in. "The asshole on the floor shot him with a revolver hidden in his desk. He'd be dead now too, except we know the laws in this state. All we wanted was some money—nobody was supposed to get hurt."

"So what's the offer?" asked the gunman in the doorway.

"Now that I know the bank manager is still alive, and if you promise not to harm anyone, you are free to leave. There's a certified letter in this case to that effect, signed by the governor—simply walk out with the paper in hand...hold it up for the news cameras that are no doubt waiting outside, if you like."

"Sounds too easy." The robber moved next to Arlo, who was still seated in the wingback chair, though now melancholy and beardless.

"Would you prefer it to be more difficult?" asked IM.

"No," replied the gunman in the doorway, "more profitable. The way I figure it, the only reason you're here is because there's something more valuable than money in this bank."

Arlo sat up slightly as he noticed IM's twitching hand. "That's very perceptive of you. In the bank's vault there is a safety deposit box that contains documents, which could prove embarrassing for some very powerful people. While you might be tempted to search for those documents yourself, there are a few things to consider. One, the vault houses over a thousand safety deposit boxes, each of which requires a bank key and a matching customer key to open. Two, the vault was remotely locked when the bank's alarm was triggered, and so now the vault door's time lock has been activated, meaning even if you did manage to negotiate for the combination, no one but the Hulk or perhaps the Human Torch would be capable of opening that door for several hours. Three, the documents have no monetary value, though certainly you could attempt to blackmail those who the documents incriminate, but as I mentioned...they're powerful people for whom, I suspect, being extorted would not sit well."

As IM spoke, with his hands down at his side, he signed in ASL letters: ARLO YOUR COMPANIONS WILL NEVER LEAVE THIS BANK FREE MEN. THEY ARE DOOMED TO DIE #UST LIKE YOUR BROTHER DYLAN UNLESS YOU DO AS I TELL YOU. THIS CASE CONTAINS A SONIC DEVICE THAT WILL MOMENTARILY INCAPACITATE ANYONE WITHIN EARSHOT EXCEPT YOU WHO WILL ONLY FIND ITS EFFECTS SOMEWHAT DI**YNG. SHOOT YOUR COMRADES WHEN IT IS ACTIVATED AND YOU HAVE MY WORD THAT YOU CAN FLEE THE BANK DISGUISED AS A HOSTAGE AS YOU HAD PLANNED. OTHERWISE YOU AND YOUR COMRADES WILL BE KILLED BY THE SWAT TEAM THAT INTENDS TO BREACH THE BANK IN LESS THAN FIVE MINUTES WHICH WILL BE FAR MESSIER AND LIKELY RESULT IN COLLATERAL DAMAGE THAT WILL BE ON YOUR HEAD.

"Can we keep the money?" asked the robber standing next to Arlo.

"Of course not," answered IM.

"Then no way," said the gunman in the doorway.

"We've got to have something to show for our trouble," added the robber who then noticed Arlo looking up at him. "And the loss of our friend."

"Give me a moment to confer with the authorities outside." IM left the channel open as he typed the words "disregard inquiry" on his touch screen. "They're asking to keep some of the money...okay, I'll inform them." IM made a clicking noise with his tongue. "If it will help expedite a resolution, you'll be allowed to leave with half."

"Half?" asked the gunman in the doorway.

"What are we supposed to do?" asked the robber near Arlo. "Count up all the money and then divide it in two...that's not going to be very expeditious."

"Ten night-deposit bags have been spotted outside the office—take five," replied IM. "Any five you wish. I assure you, everyone outside—just as I imagine everyone inside—wants all this over with. No one's going renege on the deal over a few extra dollars if you happen to take the five fullest bags."

The gunman in the doorway eyed the zippered bags stacked just outside the door, a few bulging more than the others. He nodded to Arlo and the other robber. "Okay, let 'em know we'll take the deal, but we're walking out of here with a hostage each until we get to those reporters outside and show them the paperwork signed by the governor."

"That's not necessary," said IM, "but so long as no harm befalls them it won't alter the deal."

The gunman in the doorway moved into the office and stood over the manager on the floor. "All right, get up. I pick you as my hostage, and if they start shooting I'll make you my shield."

"We'll take a couple from out there." The robber put a hand on Alro's shoulder.

"Don't forget your paperwork," said IM as he signed in ASL letters: ARLO COUGH SO THAT I KNOW YOU UNDERSTAND AND AGREE TO OUR DEAL.

The gunman pulled the bank manager off the floor by his coat collar and noticed IM's hand. "What's with your fingers? Why're they twitching like that?"

"Yeah," said the other robber. "I noticed that earlier too."

"I'm not sure, since I can't see myself, but it's likely a glitch in the holographic software," replied IM. "It sometimes struggles to fully render extremities."

Arlo coughed. The robber patted him on the back. "There's no reason to get choked up now...we're almost out of here." The robber smiled as he approached the holographic image standing atop the desk. "Just between us, are you really real?"

"I assume you're referring to that persistently circulating conspiracy theory that I'm merely some sort of artificial intelligence," IM said. "You've seen me periodically in interviews over the past few years, correct? I've aged, haven't I?"

The gunman stopped as he led the bank manager toward the office door. "But if you were CGI in the first place, then it wouldn't be no big thing to make you look a little older each year."

"That's an interesting point," said IM, "but I suggest we put this discussion in abeyance for the time being. My authenticity shouldn't concern you right now—only that the letter within this case is, indeed, authentic."

The robber removed his jacket from around the case. "How do I open this damn thing?"

"Just pull that knob I mentioned."

~ * ~

IM heard the familiar chime and looked up at the viewscreen from his protein shake. "Hello there."

"The father of the anonymous bank customer would like to thank you in person for a job well done."

"You mean he's so grateful that he intends to fly all the way to my secluded domicile and risk vectoring in pathogens in an effort to express his appreciation?" asked IM.

"No, I mean he wants to thank you virtually...but in real time."

"Please inform the senator that his unspoken gratitude is thanks enough."

"How did you know he's a...oh, never mind."

"So what happened to the deaf assailant after he shot his associates?"

"The cops corralled all the hostages as they came running out of the bank, so you didn't lie to him, which I know—for reasons I can't fathom—is important to you...he was able to egress just as he'd planned, but the manager IDed him soon after. He didn't do such a great job of shooting his comrades—got them both in the belly...neither died, but at least he incapacitated them, preventing a potential shootout, most likely saving their lives."

"I suppose all's well that ends well." IM returned his attention to his shake.

"I didn't know you knew ASL."

"Just the alphabet—I find it handier than Morse Code."

"Listen, word of your involvement in this incident was leaked to the press, and they've been breathless about it for the past several hours."

"I thought the whole point of my involvement was to keep the incident from becoming a national headline."

"Nevertheless, the media has now taken to portraying you as sort of digital-age Sherlock Holmes...a new hat they seem anxious for you to wear."

"I wear plenty of hats already; I don't want to don a deerstalker too," IM replied. "Besides, I'm like the opposite of that character. He was a sociopathic genius, and I'm just a guy brimming with empathy who happens to have a high-speed Internet connection."

"Be that as it may, I thought I'd give you a heads up, as it seems you haven't been watching the news since your involvement in said incident."

"I got caught up in a Buster Keaton retrospective." IM shook his prepackaged shake container. "Anyhow, it doesn't really matter—it's not likely that reporters will be showing up on my doorstep. By the way, break a leg during your interview tonight. I'll be watching."

Chapter Two

The talk show host addressed the studio audience from behind his desk. "Tonight's going to feel a bit like we're back in the pandemic, because I'll be interviewing my first guest via satellite. However, when you hear who the guest is, I don't think you'll be disappointed. According to Currency Affairs, the recent valuation of his now publicly traded company, of which he's the majority shareholder, has made him the world's first trillionaire. Also, I'm told he's a very capable yodeler. Please welcome, live from parts unknown, Jodian."

The host swiveled in his chair as a screen lowered over his shoulder. The decibel level of the audience's applause increased when Jodian's face appeared. Jodian smiled benevolently. "Thank you—that's very kind."

The host shook his head. "This is the first time I've seen a standing-O for somebody who's not actually in the building."

Jodian nodded. "I appreciate the special accommodations."

"And I appreciate you not buying and selling our planet," rejoined the host.

"Fixer-uppers are a hard sell these days."

"My first question is, once and for all, can you explain to me and my studio audience how a blockchain actually works? I'm just kidding, nobody cares." The host waited a moment for the laughter to subside. "Seriously though, there was a time not long ago when the thought of one person having a trillion dollars was ridiculous...I mean, it would've been easier to imagine somebody being able to breathe underwater or to fly, but you showed the world that the trick to making a trillion dollars is to simply reinvent money."

"Well," replied Jodian, "I'm only a trillionaire on paper—"

"Which is ironic," interrupted the host, "since the old money your new money is now usurping was printed on paper."

Jodian chuckled. "Yes, I suppose that is an amusing bit of irony."

"So, what are you going to spend it all on? If it were me, I'd buy like a billion oversized, super hi-def TVs and then give them away...but have them set up to only ever show this program."

"I don't think that'd be a very shrewd investment on my part."

"Of course not, you're already on practically every screen these days—right now, for our home viewers, you're on a screen within a screen. Me...I have to act like a clown to get each viewer I have." Once again, the host paused while the laughter abated. "Let me ask you—and I know this is a big question for a late-night talk show like mine—do you think it's fair or ethical or whatever word you want to use for one person to have so much money?"

"In a word, no," Jodian answered. "They say I'm worth a million times more than the average middle-aged professional—that's patently absurd. I'm certainly not a million times smarter than your average engineer, and I definitely don't work a million times harder than your average teacher, so I shouldn't be a million times richer."

"My first instinct is to say, then why not give it all away, but of course we're all aware of your very generous philanthropy work...especially with those who are immunocompromised such as yourself."

"Thank you...obviously, I have a special relationship with that community, but my foundation also funds a number—"

"Yes, of course," the host interrupted. "I believe just about every major city has some sort of healthcare facility named after you, but I want to get back to what you were saying before about not deserving so much money."

"Well, I didn't say that exactly. Afterall, pro-ball players shouldn't make a hundred times that of a P.E. teacher, but that's not quite the same as saying they don't deserve it...they are the best at what they do."

"So then you see yourself as the best at what you do...whatever that is?"

"At this moment, yes...or someone else would be in my place

tonight."

"That's a fair point. I don't think our show has any intention of booking the world's second-most-successful cryptocurrency entrepreneur."

Jodian smiled. "I wouldn't...he's a bit of a slippery character."

"So then back to you giving all your money away...your net worth is greater than that of most countries. Why not, as some have suggested, simply pay yourself a paltry salary of say a hundred million dollars a year and give the rest of your money to the government so it can fund all those social programs that we all agree are a good idea but that the taxpayers can't afford?"

"Firstly, my wants are pretty simple. I eschew fancy foods and expensive luxuries, so I assure you that I could live quite comfortably on much less than the salary you proposed. Secondly, what I pay to the government in taxes is substantial. I'm not complaining, mind you, but I have the sense that some people think the superrich get out of paying taxes, and it just isn't so...maybe we should be made to pay even more—I'm not debating that, but we already pay a lot."

"I can attest to that," said the host. "But I think many people are still smarting from the whole concept of Trickledown Economics—what a branding blunder that was—which seems to resurface every other decade or so like bellbottom jeans. Anyway, please continue enumerating why what I suggested is a bad idea."

"Thirdly and finally, if I surrendered my fortune to the government, I suspect it would only be squandered—either by, speaking of taxes, politicians self-servingly giving their constituents a reprieve from paying taxes for a few years all but guarantying their reelection, which might seem like a fine thing to do—no one likes paying taxes, but would a three year hiatus from taxes vastly improve the lives of most people? Maybe, though by and large I think the majority of taxpayers would use the extra money to just buy nicer cars or take a couple of extra vacations. Alternatively, and somehow this seems a less likely scenario—though a no less inefficient reallocation of resources—maybe my money would be used to fund all those important social programs that no one actually wants to pay for. Okay, that sounds good, but let me ask you this, have you ever been summoned for jury duty? Did you feel your time in court was an efficient expenditure of human capital? Perhaps never having to serve in that capacity is the lone benefit of being on permanent home confinement."

"It's the only upside I can think of for being a convicted felon," added the host.

"Right...and how about at the post office or the DMV? Are there many, or any, government institutions that you can confidently point to and say, 'Yeah that works—they really know what they're doing there?' I already spend most of my money—and I fully intend to keep doing so—on programs that I believe benefit our society, but I do so in a precise and results-driven manner. At the risk of sounding immodest, who do you think is better equipped to decide how all my money gets spent; a guy whose only birthright was a weakened immune system who went on to invent new technologies and worked his way up from nothing to become a trillionaire, or a bunch of bureaucrats who never seem to agree on anything and can't ever balance a budget?"

The host set his coffee mug on his desk. "If you start badmouthing politicians, I can't imagine anybody's going to disagree with you. As my third wife's divorce lawyer used to quip, 'I ain't saying you're right, but you ain't far wrong.' So tell me, when he's not disrupting global economies and changing the face of modern finance, what does the world's richest man enjoy doing in his leisure time?"

"I'm really a pretty boring guy...I don't get out much."

The host took another sip of coffee as the audience laughed. "You've certainly expanded the definition of working from home. Do you like playing video games in your spare time...are you a gamer? Tell the world your screenname...I bet it's Buttcoin."

Jodian grinned and shook his head. "No, I never really got into that scene. I like to build models during my downtime."

"Like airplanes?"

"Mostly things that soar a bit higher, like rocket ships and satellites."

"I've got to tell you, I have a hard time picturing you sitting at your coffee table, gluing together popsicle sticks to make Sputnik 2.0."

"Everyone needs a hobby," replied Jodian.

"I figured the hobby of somebody with your kind of money would be collecting a fleet of superyachts."

"If you pride yourself on the things you buy rather than the things you make, then you have little to be proud of."

"Ending your sentence with a preposition, just like us common folk. You've shown us tonight that you're somebody who really knows how to find the 'fun' in fungible funds. Thank you so much for being here with us this evening...well, almost. Let's give it up for Jodian. Stay tuned for tonight's musical guest, The Shave Bumps."

Chapter Three

IM logged into the Snowbound dating website and clicked the chat button. He had a message waiting for him from Eileen88. He typed a response: *E, are you still there?*

A spinning clock appeared above Eileen's avatar. *Yes, S, I just messaged you a moment ago. I wasn't sure if you'd be on tonight.*

We've been messaging every night for nearly a year.

And each night when I logon, I expect tonight to be the night I never hear from you again.

That's awfully cynical, E. Have I given you any reason not to trust me?

You're a man, right? That's reason enough.

You sound like you're in a mood. Everything okay?

The spinning clock reappeared then disappeared again. *My ex brought his new girlfriend to our daughter's recital tonight...they're practically the same age.*

Ouch. IM sipped a juice box as he considered what else to write. *I'm sure him dating a younger woman has more to do with his age than yours.*

You're probably right. It just would've been nice if you were in the seat next to me instead of my crutches.

I'm certain your medical condition will improve before mine...in fact, it already has. I'd give anything to be able to go out on crutches.

Sorry, I didn't mean for this to turn into a pity party featuring me. Having spent the better part of the past year as a shut-in wasn't so bad since most everyone else was quarantining because of the latest wave of this interminable pandemic, but now that the restrictions are being lifted, this last month of trying to hobble around in public has...well, I guess it's true what they say about misery loving company.

You've always got me...I'm not going anywhere.

But that's not the same as having you, is it? At least not the way I want.

IM tilted his head back before responding. *What are you trying to tell me, E?*

Chatting with you this year has been wonderful. It's really been a bright spot for me during this dark period of my life. If not for you, I don't know how I would've gotten through the divorce and the car accident.

I'm still here for you. If we were good together during the dark times, think how great the sunnier days ahead could be.

Those pictures you emailed me—I did an Internet search. They're of some guy who lives in Illinois. He's married with two kids.

My apologies for the thin lie. It was so nice of you to send me pictures, and it seemed important that I reciprocate. He's not me.

I know. Against my better judgment I contacted him. That was a mistake. He, of course, had no idea who I was, so it was an uncomfortable conversation to say the least. Are you actually immunocompromised like you told me? Are you even real?

Again, I apologize. The truth is that I'm a somewhat recognizable person, and I didn't want my celebrity status to interfere in any way with our evolving relationship. You help me feel more down-to-earth.

Stop! I've heard enough lies for one lifetime. S, even though you weren't always straight with me, I know we shared something special. I'm sorry for all your troubles...health and otherwise. I hope my ending this—whatever it was—doesn't add to them, but I need more. This is too thin a life for me. I wish you all the best.

E, can I at least know your real name?

So long Solitaire71.

Chapter Four

IM heard the familiar chime and muted the movie he was watching, taking note of the time. "Hello there."

"I noticed your light was on."

"I'm finishing The Postman Always Rings Twice, the second movie in a film noir double feature."

"What was the first feature?"

"Double Indemnity," answered IM. "Any particular reason you called?"

"Nah...just figured you were the only one I knew who was still up."

"I never seem to maintain a regular sleep schedule."

"Did you catch my interview tonight?" asked Jodian.

"Yeah, I liked the new Shave Bumps song...had a good hook."

"No notes about yours truly?"

"You're like a different person on those things, but I thought you did fine—didn't come across as...well, you know how the press sometimes portrays you."

"You and me both...imagine the field day the media would have if they ever discovered that we're brothers."

"I'm sure they'd be shocked to learn that you're related to someone so handsome and intelligent."

"That's a humorous thing to say. What's wrong with you? The only time you're funny is when you're depressed."

"A woman I'd been dating broke up with me earlier tonight."

"If my arithmetic is correct, she's the fourth gal in the past month."

"Yes, though the second one was a guy," IM replied, "but she was the last of them...the last connection I'd made since I started online dating a year ago."

"Tough break...but still, where'd you expect your relationships to go? I know you're not the type to ghost anyone, but at some point they're going to want to cuddle—whatever that is."

"I suppose...but it felt nice to be involved in someone else's life—made me feel more...I don't know, maybe just more. Twice today someone asked me if I was real."

"Would I have spent what it cost to install you in your own, private space station if you weren't real?"

"Space station sounds a bit hyperbolic," said IM. "Space pod, seems more accurate."

"Fine, but what I spend to ferry up your supplies—that's real. Otherwise, instead of moving about your floating dorm room, you'd be confined to a hospital bed like you were for the first couple decades of your life with only the vaguest notion of consciousness."

"I know...you needn't constantly remind me. I appreciate the special treatment, even if I don't happen to mention it every single time we chat, but I'd be glad to share this high-rise studio apartment of mine with a roommate. Has your foundation made any headway finding someone who's similarly afflicted?"

"I'm afraid not. Statistically speaking, they must be out there, but as you know it's nearly impossible in most parts of the world for a baby who's severely immunocompromised to be identified early enough to take the necessary measures to enhance the likelihood of long-term viability...add a rare cardiovascular condition such as yours and the chances of a child surviving to his or her first birthday is exceptionally low. You just happened to possess the good fortune of having an older brother who's similarly afflicted, putting our team of doctors on alert for potential complications—but we'll continue the search."

"I hate to think of someone being cursed like me," said IM, "but if anyone is...well, as I was reminded earlier tonight, misery loves company."

"Your dual disorders make you uniquely qualified to be a long-term denizen of space, and lately I've been thinking that perhaps that's not such a bad place to live."

"Not the 'it isn't a curse, it's a gift' pep talk again."

"I sincerely believe you may represent the next stage in human evolution, destined to outlive all the rest of us on this planet we continue to foul."

"If your plan is for me to repropagate the species, then I think I'm going to need a partner. I promise, I'm not all that particular...the Bride of Frankenstein would do."

"You're still a young man...you have time. Nothing would please me more than sending you up some company. If my doctors thought I could survive the journey, I might even pay you a visit myself."

IM shook his head. "The world needs you on terra firma, even if no one quite knows where you are. There are those who think, perhaps rightly so, that society cannot evolve if a few are placed too highly above all the rest. Should the planet's populace ever discover that you were floating above them the way I am now, well...you'd never be able to shake your reputation of being a condescending elitist."

"Right, the optics of that could present a challenge." Jodian yawned. "Listen, it's been a long day for me, so I'm going to turn in for the night, but since you're still up, would you mind taking another little assignment...sort of a favor for a friend type thing? It's a job that's impossible to mess up—the ultimate outcome is already assured, and you seem to be in a chatty mood anyway."

Chapter Five

The night nurse in the dementia ward knocked on the door of the room at the end of the corridor. "Ms. Delfy, is everything okay?"

"Go away," replied a small voice from within.

"In a minute, but I'm doing my final round. It's time for lights out, and I can see light coming from under your door."

The nurse heard movement on the other side of the door as the light from below disappeared. "I turned out the damn light. Now leave me alone."

"Ms. Delfy, I'll leave you to your privacy as soon as you turn out your light. I can still see that the light's on through the peephole."

The pinpoint of light shining through the door went dark. "Stop being such a Peeping Tom."

"My name's not Tom, and no one is peeping at you, but I can hear you just on the other side of the door. I think you're covering the peephole with your finger and the light's still on in there. You need your sleep, Ms. Delfy."

"What for?"

The night nurse sighed. "To maintain your sunny disposition."

"Go to hell."

"Ms. Delfy, I know you don't mean that. Please turn off your light and go to bed. You can watch TV if you want so long as you keep the volume low, but it's time for lights out.

"Fine."

The light under the door reappeared as did the light through the peephole. The nurse heard footsteps cross the small room followed by the flick of a switch. The light from within went out, then the quiet sound of cable news came on. "I'll be at the front desk, so buzz me if you need anything."

"I'd like to buzz you right upside your head."

"Goodnight, Ms. Delfy."

~ * ~

Ms. Delfy pulled the covers up to her neck as she watched a woman wearing too much makeup talk about forest fires and other calamities in California. *This bimbo looks like a cross between a prostitute and a corpse.* Of late, Ms. Delfy struggled to tell TV personalities apart despite still vaguely recognizing them, so she'd taken to assuming that everyone on television was someone she'd seen before and had been disappointed by. She changed the channel and another talking head appeared—this time a man who likewise looked somewhat familiar.

"Ms. Delfy?" asked IM tentatively. "Am I pronouncing your name correctly?"

She changed the channel again. *Commercials have gotten so strange...used to be they showed you a product and then explained why you couldn't live without it. Now most of the time I don't even know what the hell they're trying to sell me.* The same talking head reappeared.

"Ms. Delfy, I apologize for the intrusion. I promise I can't see or hear you, but could you tap the menu button on your TV's remote control to confirm that you in fact can see and hear me?"

She skeptically pressed the menu button on her remote. "It's asking me if I want to adjust the picture settings."

"Thank you for confirming that you can see me on your television, Ms. Delfy."

"But I can't—the menu screen is blocking you."

"Incidentally, if you find yourself stuck in the menu, just hit the exit button. I do a lot of TV watching myself, so I know how difficult those menus can sometimes be to navigate."

She did as instructed. "There you are."

"I imagine you're wondering if I'm some sort of commercial spokesman, like Mr. Clean or the Brawny paper towel guy perhaps."

"You're too scrawny for either of them."

"I assure you that I'm not attempting to sell you anything. Your son, with whom I understand you're estranged, asked a friend of his if I would contact you."

"My son died decades ago...didn't he?"

"You're probably asking how I managed to infiltrate your television. You see, your rest home receives a satellite signal that is then disaggregated among each of the TVs in...okay, I see now that you're pressing the menu button repeatedly, so I take it that I'm not actually answering your question...and that maybe you're a little bit impatient at times. I suppose if I was as close to the end of my life's journey as you are, I'd prefer for people to get right to the point and not waste time answering unasked questions. I assume, since you don't have an open line of communication with your son, you'd like to know why he wanted me to contact you. Frankly, I have no idea. I don't know him, and I don't know you, so I suppose that makes me something of an intermediary, though one without a message to convey."

"The medium is the message," said Ms. Delfy.

"However, were I to hazard a guess, I'd say this might be an instance of the medium being the message. What I mean by that is your son called in quite a favor for me to be with you this evening—no mean feat, I promise you. Speaking of feet, forgive the pun, if mine were in your slippers I'd interpret my presence as an olive branch of sorts...think of me as a bridge builder or a fence mender, although I never quite understood that last idiom since fences are meant to keep people apart."

"You're veering into pointlessness."

"Listening to myself just now, I sound as if I have no point," said IM. "Maybe I don't, but from what I read in your dossier, you seem like a very independent woman. Now, I imagine, a lot of that independence has been taken from you. I can relate."

"Is that right, Mr. I Can Get Into Anyone's TV Set I damn well please?"

"Ironically perhaps, my image can travel via satellite signals to almost anywhere in the world, and yet I'm isolated in a room that's probably about the same size of yours. The difference is that I'm never allowed to leave. I also perused your medical records. I too am familiar with the mind addling effects of dizziness or fainting spells. I frequently suffered similar symptoms as an adolescent. My doctors were concerned that my poorly functioning arteries might soon cease to send blood to my brain. They told me it was a miracle that I'd lived through my childhood, which due to my condition, I remember very little of."

Ms. Delfy wiped her eyes. "The worst thing about forgetting is that you know who you are, but you don't know why."

"Unpleasant though they must've been, the unfortunate part of not remembering my formative years is that I don't understand how I became the way I am now, but I have found recently that creative writing helps me shore up the lacunas. I don't really know if my writing is based on experiences I can't quite recall or if the characters are composites of people that've been a part of the forgotten times in my life. However, the process of creating fills in the holes to make me feel, well, more whole...at least for a little while. Would you like to hear the latest scene from a play I've been writing?"

Ms. Delfy pressed the menu button on her remote.

Chapter Six

What Rad liked most about his creative writing class was also what he liked least—the time spent away from the tedium of the rest of his day. He looked forward to the twice-weekly class, but it always seemed to end before it ever really got started and then it was back to the inevitable drudgery, feeling all the more drudging due to the brief respite. Most of the short stories written by his classmates were in the confessional style, and certainly many of these authors were long overdue for some confessing, but the regrets expressed in their writing primarily had to do with missed opportunities; not taking advantage of some chance they'd been given long ago, forgoing to learn something new that seemed monotonous at the time, or quitting a sport because the practices had been too hard. Sometimes it could be revelatory, but to Rad most of it felt self-indulgent.

A hand shot up from a desk in the second row. The MFA candidate from the local university standing at the front of the classroom nodded. "Remember, you don't have to raise your hand to ask a question in here. You can just ask it."

They young man lowered his hand. "Right, my bad. So in the story I'm working on, I'm going to write about visits with my pops when I was just a tyke. I spent every other Sunday afternoon with him. Should I use the word biweekly? I'm not sure if it means twice a week or once every two weeks?"

The instructor adjusted his glasses. "Well, it can mean either, but if you're unsure of a word's meaning then it's a good bet your reader will be too, so I would write it the way you just explained it to me— every other Sunday."

"Yeah, I hear you," said the young man, "but shouldn't my writing be...you know, fancier than the way I talk?"

"It depends on the kind of story you want to write."

"It's a story about how my pops used to teach me the best ways to boost cars and shit."

"Okay," said the instructor, "that's interesting, but while biweekly boosting has a nice alliteration to it, I think I'd still stick with every other Sunday."

The young man shook his head. "But it's about more than that too. Like even though he was a terrible father, and it's messed up to teach a kid how to hotwire a car, those are good memories, so I want to make them sound special...fancy-like."

The instructor rubbed the stubble on his chin. "How about using the word 'fortnightly'?"

The young man scribbled a note on his pad of paper with alacrity. "Yo, that's fire."

Ram had grown weary of the young man's maudlin stories over the past few weeks. This was blackout pod 1A after all—the elite of society's lowest caste, the best of the dregs. He thought more should be expected of its inmates than overstated sentimentality. "Enough with the little daddy's boy story. I don't know what they taught you in pod 2B before you transferred...the way I figure it, they pulled you out cuz they thought you were due to get cleaned up for being such a wuss. Don't go thinking we're soft in here just cuz we do some creative writing; you could learn a thing or two about being a man from my joints. The story I'm working on has it all—sex and violence and sex." Every class has a clown and a bully; Ram was the latter. "Whose turn is it to read for our next class?"

The instructor consulted his notes. "It looks like Conrad is reading next time."

Ram threw up his hands. "Ugh, I'm sick of his spaceman stories. They don't even make no sense."

"A story not making sense and a story not making sense to you are two very different things," said Rad.

Several students teetered on the verge of laughter. "What's that supposed to be...like some kind of joke," asked Ram.

"No, what's a joke is your writing," Rad clowned. "I'm not sure any of us can stomach another one of your stories about you pulling off the crime of the century, during which you have improbable sex just before eluding the police."

"You sayin' my stories are made up?"

"Well, this is a fiction writing class...in a prison."

The instructor raised an arm for calm. "All right gentlemen, that's enough. Okay class, when next we meet, we'll have Conrad read the latest installment from his novel in progress, after which we'll offer constructive and considerate critiques while discussing any concerns or questions we might have about our own writing in the process." The instructor nodded to the guard standing in the doorway as the students collected their things and lined up to leave. "Conrad, can you hang on a moment?"

Rad approached the instructor as the others exited the classroom in a single-file line. "Hey, I wasn't trying to start something with Ram and disrespect your class or nothing like that. I just didn't like the way he talked down to Tyke."

"No, I didn't like it either, so I appreciate you stepping in, though be careful—that's a big dude. Incidentally, I'm not concerned about you disrespecting my class. We live on opposite sides of these walls, but otherwise I think you and I are a lot alike. We're about the same age, we both have a talent for writing, and each of us is anxious for our present to be in the past. Who knows, we might've been grad students together if you'd been born into different circumstances." The instructor pulled several pages from his satchel. "Anyway, I wanted to give you these."

Rad accepted the pages and glanced at the red ink in the margins. "This is my first chapter from *Plausible Faces*...but you already gave me feedback on this."

"Those aren't my comments. I took the liberty of submitting it to a literary journal."

"And they want to publish an excerpt?"

The instructor latched his satchel and slung the strap over his shoulder. "No, but don't be discouraged. I sent that same journal three of my short stories before they finally published one...and as you'll notice the editor took the time to write some notes. They only do that when they think your writing has potential, and they want to see more of it."

Rad rolled up the papers into a tight baton. "I'll review what the editor had to say—thanks."

"You bet. I should let you go catch up to the others, but Conrad, you have a gift—don't squander it by getting your head bashed in during some stupid fistfight out in the yard or whatever."

Chapter Seven

IM sat in front of his domicile's viewscreen, typing responses on his wireless keyboard to some of the questions in the comments section as he waited for the high school students in the classroom of the teacher hosting the video call to decide whose turn it was next.

"IM, do you drink?" asked a student with skin that puberty had not been kind to.

"Quite often," answered IM, "mostly teas and protein shakes."

"No...I mean alcohol."

"I never drink that poison, do you?"

"I drink beer on occasion," answered the young man, "and those occasions are called weekends."

"I'm reporting your malfeasance to your local police department as we speak," replied IM with a straight face. "I'm confident that your new reform school will help you to better focus on your studies."

The students in the classroom laughed as some of the students watching online posted strings of uninterpretable emoticons.

"No," the acne-riddled student mock-pleaded, "don't sic the lice-lice on me."

"Lice-lice?" asked IM. "I'm not familiar with that term."

The young man smiled. "You know how some people say 'po-po' when they mean police...well, I like to say lice-lice instead."

IM nodded. "That's fascinating...and when I say 'fascinating' I mean absolute balderdash."

"What kind of tea do you drink?" asked another student after her classmates stopped laughing. "I'm guessing an exotic oolong."

IM grinned. "Close. It's a special blend...Lipton over ice with a little sugar mixed in."

The teacher pointed to a student in the back of the classroom who'd raised her hand. "IM, do you have a girlfriend?"

IM sipped iced tea through the straw of his thermos as he waited for the giggles to die down. "That question hardly ever gets asked...more than once during each of these teen chat sessions. By the way, I don't care for the term girlfriend. Gal pal or lady friend would seem more appropriate. Let me ask the young women in the class and online— doesn't being called a girl feel a bit condescending?"

The student who'd asked the question nodded. "I hadn't thought of that before, but I guess it kind of does. So what would you suggest us gals call our boyfriends?"

"I submit for your consideration the term guy buddies," answered IM. "I'm a fan of the blues, and I especially enjoy Buddy Guy's music, so I'd think it pretty cool if a lady called me her guy buddy."

"I like the sound of that too, though you didn't really answer my question. Do you have a gal pal?"

"Or are you gay?" blurted out the weekend beer drinker.

IM shook his head. "I don't know what I am, frankly. It's like asking someone who's been a vegetarian his entire life if he prefers steak to lobster. I imagine most of you have more experience in that domain than I do."

"I know I do," said the young man.

"That's fascinating, and I think you know what I really mean by that." IM read an instant message from his brother as the classroom erupted into laughter all over again. "Listen, I'm sorry to cut our time together short, but it looks like there's an emergent situation that requires my immediate attention."

A young woman stood up. "Wait, before you go, I'm a writer for the school newspaper, and I know there's like a one percent chance that you'll actually answer this, but if you did it'd be the scoop of the century for my paper, not to mention automatic acceptance into the journalism college of my choice, so here goes: where do you live?"

"Young lady, in life you'll find there are some situations that have a one percent chance of success, but a great many more situations that come with a hundred percent chance of regret if you don't put forth the effort. The two questions I get asked most often are the one you just posed and 'What does IM stand for?' to which my typical cagey answer is: truth and forthrightness; however, you demonstrated courage in the asking, so I'll answer your query without equivocation. Honestly, I live all around the world. I move about quite a lot, frequently relocating under the cover of darkness. I should go now, but it was a pleasure talking with you all."

IM clicked the End Call button, and the waving teenagers on his screen vanished, replaced by the visage of his brother. "I caught the last little bit of your confab...cute stuff. I didn't realize you were so popular with juveniles."

IM shrugged. "Apparently, I have what's known as 'sway' or 'rizz' in the adolescent argot. It seems they relate to me...perhaps because we're all exposed to way too much screentime."

"Let's hope you have the same sway with baggage handlers. Negotiations at Orchard International have been stalled for weeks."

"I've been following the situation on the news."

"Well, the new news is that the union is about to walk from the table. If the baggage handlers strike, it'll effectively shut down the largest hub in the Midwest, which would have cascading global repercussions, all at a time when the precarious airline industry can least afford them."

IM nodded. "Yes, as I mentioned, I watch the news...quite frequently in fact."

"I'm so pleased that you're abreast of the current state of affairs. The union has agreed to stay at the table a little longer if you call in personally. It seems the one thing both sides can agree on is that having you act as an emergency arbitrator would be beneficial, which makes sense to me since choosing you over a professional arbitrator seems downright arbitrary—they might as well have picked whoever's atop the Billboard Hot 100 this week—but then I doubt the union really believes you'll make the call. You're being patched through to the conference room, and you're on speaker phone...now."

"Good..." IM thought for a moment, "...afternoon, I believe it is there."

"What time is it where you are?" a woman in a business suit

asked.

"The same—half past the hour, so it would seem we've managed to find some common ground already, which I believe qualifies as an auspicious start. First, let me see if I have a clear understanding of the situation. Over the last couple of decades, being an airline pilot has become a less desirable vocation than it once was, ascribable in part to ever more stressful schedules, so a decreased number of prospective pilots are entering the field, while at the same time there's been an increased demand due to record growth in air travel, which has raised their wages. During those selfsame decades, being a flight attendant has become a less desirable vocation than it once was, ascribable in part to ever more unruly passengers, so a decreased number of prospective attendants are entering the field, while at the same time there's been an increased demand due to record growth in air travel, which has raised their wages. Meanwhile, what's required to attract prospective baggage handlers has remained more or less the same. While record growth in air travel has increased the number of handlers that are necessary for an airport to function, heretofore there has been a steady supply of new applicants to meet those demands as being a baggage handler doesn't require extensive training like an airline pilot or a unique temperament like a flight attendant, so wages have remained relatively flat."

"And it's not fair," said a man with a mustache. "Our job is as important as theirs. Those suitcases don't load themselves."

"I think you're correct," replied IM. "Fairness is what's really at issue here. From what I understand, the airlines have offered a sizeable wage increase over your last contract—"

"Yeah," the mustachioed man interrupted, "but it's not nearly as big a percentage as the pilots and flight attendants got when they threatened to strike."

IM chuckled. "That's exactly what I was about to say before your interruption."

"Sorry, these last few weeks have been frustrating...filled with lots of interrupting."

"You can underline lots," added the woman in the suit.

"Yes, I've been party to many meetings like this in recent years,"

IM replied. "Always makes me somewhat thankful that I'm not there in the same room. Anyway, I don't want to waste your time or mine, so let's get to it. I see on my screen here that the latest offer on the table is for a fifteen percent pay bump, and the counter was a fifty percent increase. There's a great deal of distance between those two numbers. Distance can be a funny thing, especially how it can influence our perspective. It puts me in mind of the water strider...you know, the little insect that lives on the surface of a pond. Think how big its world must seem, free to move all around a still pond. Then one day perhaps it notices a bird flying overhead, and the next a frog jumping out of the water onto the bank, then the next a fish swimming below, and suddenly its world feels very small even though nothing about the pond has changed."

The businesswoman coughed. "Sorry, that sounds like the start of a really interesting Zen koan or something, but you mentioned not wanting to waste our time."

"Yeah," the man with the mustache agreed, "and we don't appreciate being compared to bugs."

IM sighed. "I assure you that I meant no insult to anyone, though you might take umbrage at what I have to say next. Handling baggage doesn't merit a fifty percent pay raise—not today."

The mustachioed man pounded his fist on the table. "Why the hell not? Vacations are a lot less fun if you have to wear the same clothes every damn day. Do you think the pilots are going to start tossing suitcases into the cargo hold before takeoff? Our jobs are way more important than that of the stewardesses who just dole out sodas."

IM shook his head slowly. "We all know flight attendants do more than that, but I understand you're trying to make a point, though what you fail to understand is that you've already made it. More money is always nice, but what this stalled negotiation really comes down to, I believe, is respect. The baggage handlers feel disrespected when they look up from the tarmac under the belly of the plane and see the well-dressed pilots and crew exchanging pleasantries with the passengers, while your efforts go largely unnoticed until a mistake is made.

However, the reality is that while your job is as important as a pilot, it doesn't require years of flight school. While baggage handlers are just as integral as flight attendants, the job doesn't need the rarefied skillset of being able to deal with belligerent drunks while simultaneously trying to calm nervous flyers. But you want to be respected equally, since undoubtedly you work just as hard as them—quite reasonable. What's not reasonable is a fifty percent pay hike. I suspect the airlines are close to simply letting all of you go and hiring contract workers to replace you. Sure, they won't do your job as well, but customers are more likely to accept misrouted bags than flights canceled due to a protracted strike, and maybe the expense of paying the contract companies who'll find these new baggage handlers will cost a little more, but the handlers themselves will be paid considerably less. However, the upside for the airlines is that all this goes away—no more threats of work stoppages, at least from all of you. And should the contractors ever go on strike themselves, then the airlines will just look for a new contract company, one more adept at keeping its people in line, an unpleasant prospect for all the workers involved."

"So then what do you suggest?" asked the mustached man.

"Take the fifteen percent, and then ask for two percent more," IM answered.

"What can seventeen percent buy that fifteen can't?" the man asked.

"Respect," answered IM. "People respect generosity. Donate that extra two percent of all the baggage handlers' pay to charity and ask the pilots and flight attendants to match your donation. Some will and some won't, but because you make less than them, your generosity will serve as an inspiration. Invite all those who donate to help decide how the money will be distributed—might I suggest Honor Flights or some other aviation-themed cause. You'll hold meetings that your union will host, since after all pilots and flight attendants are often away from home, but baggage handlers remain in town when your shifts are over, so you'll be available to organize everything. Voila...you have your seat at the table, which you get the credit for having set."

The mustachioed man let out a low whistle. "And I doubt the airlines would be as likely to push us around if we headed up an organization with that kind of clout."

"I'd say that's a fairly safe assumption," replied the woman in the suit.

Chapter Eight

Dear Dumbass,

I read your comments regarding the first chapter of my novel, which was submitted to your publication without my consent. I've never heard of you and know nothing about your so-called literary journal, except to say that if you're the publisher then the paper it's printed on would be better used as prison toilet tape. I suggest you pulp any future edition of your rag that may currently be at the printing press and immediately retire to some remote part of the world where no one reads, speaks, or has even heard of the English language. Your unsolicited opinions only serve the cause of stupidity.

Since my current situation affords me an inordinate amount of free time and because it amuses me to do so, I will address your notes in turn, though I have no expectation that you are actually intelligent enough to glean anything from my critique of your criticisms. As I embark on this undertaking, I feel as an aspiring primatologist might when tasked with teaching sign language to a particularly dim-witted orangutan, but I will do my best to edify. However, I know all I can reasonably hope for is that you refrain from playing with your feces whilst we go through these motions.

At the bottom of the first page, you wrote (and I believe as we commence that a compliment is in order for you electing to use a pen rather than the crayons that you are no doubt more comfortable with): "Aside from his unusual living situation, I find this character a little derivative." Derivative of what exactly? My protagonist is unlike any character that I have encountered in my recent years of fiction reading, and I happen to hold the distinction of checking out more books from our facility's library than all of the other scholars in my cohort.

In the margin on page two, you wrote: "I'm intrigued by your premise of describing the world as it is and presuming that the reader is somehow oblivious to what is now so commonplace, though I think some readers might find it off-putting or perhaps even insulting." No sir, it is I who am insulted. The only presumption I made of any potential readers is that they wouldn't be complete imbeciles incapable of distinguishing fiction from reality.

At the top of page three, you wrote: "This all seems to be a rather original take on an unoriginal concept." I'll tell you what's unoriginal, a hack discovering that he has an affinity for art but no artistic talent, and so he switches roles in his chosen field, transitioning from creator to critic. You wouldn't know an original thought if it crawled up your ass and established residency inside your colon, which I assume is the organ that you do most of your thinking with. Furthermore, every story is a variation of another that came before it in some way; the stories we read today are what connects us to our ancestors who told stories around a campfire. Unoriginal concepts, such as loneliness and isolation, are the very through line that connects us all throughout space and time.

And finally, you wrote on the last page: "This author has a voice that readers may find engaging, but he lacks an adequate understanding of the current state of our human condition." Oh really? Firstly, I submit that your understanding of our human condition suffers from an acute case of idiocy. Secondly, readers may find my "voice" engaging—that makes no sense. Do you also happen to think that listeners might enjoy the font I selected, or perhaps smellers would like the scent of my syntax? Thirdly, you may have more years under your belt than me, but for better or worse I've lived a full life in my three decades, and what I've learned in that time is that when insipid gatekeepers such as yourself decide who others should read, it's inevitably someone living a gilded life that personifies your narrow conception of the human condition, which so far as I can tell is predicated on a celebration of self-loathing and a generalized contempt for one's contemporaries.

In closing, I'd like to thank you for confirming what I've long suspected: to be deemed elite enough to write for any pretentious publication, one must be both mindful of uncommon criteria and forgetful of common sense. Your betters are all around you and your efforts, such as they are, are an affront to rationality.

With the utmost sincerity,
Conrad: Prisoner #655321 of Blackout Pod 1A

Chapter Nine

The director watched his actors rehearse from the fifth row as they worked through the blocking for the new scene. The lead crossed downstage as the others ambled toward the wings to take five. "Alan, I can't tell if my character is supposed to like his prison's creative writing instructor because he's taken an interest in me, or if I think he's a jerk for being a better version of myself."

Alan turned to the open laptop perched on the seat next to his. "What do you think, IM?"

IM tilted his head from side to side on the screen. "I think it's both. He appreciates the opportunity to have a creative outlet, but he probably wishes the guy was more of a father figure than a brother who's winning—know what I mean?"

The lead shook his head. "Not really. My mom was a single-parent, and I'm an only child."

"Shocking," said an actor upstage. Several other of the castmates sniggered.

Alan waved his hands above his head. "All right everyone, that's enough for today. Go learn your new lines, and we'll figure out the rest of the blocking tomorrow."

The lead rolled up the script pages as he made his way to the wings. "Great, that'll leave us with two whole days to prep before we have to perform this new scene in front of an audience. Maybe with all the leftover rehearsal time we can run improv scenarios in case anyone forgets their lines."

Alan turned the laptop toward him and tilted the screen. "Don't mind him. It just means he cares about his role and wants to perform it well."

"Could it also have anything to do with the latest review in

Theatre Digest?" asked IM.

"There's no denying that it's easier to be an actor when the thing you're acting in gets good notices. So you read the Digress review? I didn't realize that rag was even on your radar. Don't worry about what they had to say. They don't even know how to spell theater."

"Yes, the critic's assertion that our play has second act issues sort of undermines her credibility."

Alan grinned. "Why, because hitherto your play has consisted of a single, albeit ever-evolving, act?"

"That would be the reason, but still it's not so much that I care what she thinks; it's that many of the theatergoers who read her review will start thinking the same thing. Most people don't know the difference between a good play and a bad play until someone, wrong or right, points it out for them."

"I don't disagree with you, but I think the audiences may've already made up their minds. Tickets sales are slumping, and subscriptions are trending down, not to mention the actors are becoming restive about constantly learning new lines and the uncertainty of where the story is going."

IM winced. "I thought that was part of the fun for them?"

"Fun is a funny thing...like happiness, it's rarely experienced outside the confines of the ephemeral. In the long-term it settles into contentedness, and then contentment transitions into contempt, not because the situation has gotten worse, but because it hasn't changed. Humans tend toward the dynamic, and often it's their opinions that do the changing."

"But the play is always changing, since we're constantly swapping out old scenes for the new ones."

Alan shook his head. "Somehow constant change, over time, feels the same as no change, and there's rarely enough excitement to be found in a static state of affairs. A wife gets bored with her husband bringing home roses every evening, so he starts getting her different flowers each day only to sense her increasing boredom, when instead he should've just stopped buying her flowers in the first place except for the rare occasion."

"So, you think I should stop writing new scenes?"

Alan sighed. "I'm not sure. I don't think you're doing anything wrong. It's just that audiences were curious about a play written by the Immeasurable Man, curious about a story that continually evolved, but now it seems their curiosity has been sated. *Mysolation* will always be an intriguing dramaturgical experiment, but for right now people are no longer intrigued by it. I'm still amazed that someone of your elevation could write a story that's so grounded, but the reviewer has a point when she says our show seems too quotidian...that most of us feel every day the way the prisoners on the stage do. It would seem that theatergoers have decided that a prison story isn't the most manifold of metaphors for someone who spends his life in extreme isolation, but if your goal was to show a connection with the hoi polloi, then you've succeeded. Bravo."

"I thought I was writing a play that gave people hope, but perhaps I was the one who needed hope, and maybe it's just not that good. I feel as if I'm expected to write something tricky to understand to get the critics' attention—who see like five plays every week—but not so tricky as to be incomprehensible for general audiences, most of whom probably only see two plays a year, all while being unique enough that it's not too conventional but still familiar enough so it doesn't seem like it's coming out of leftfield, whatever the hell that means."

Alan rubbed his temple. "Years ago, there was an insane asylum behind leftfield where the Cubs used to play before they moved the team to Wrigley Field. The inmates would yell crazy things out the windows—that's where the phrase comes from. Anyway, I think you've unwittingly cracked the formula for success in this nutty business of pretense and pretend, which is more than what most playwrights ever manage, so don't give up and don't get down. We had a good run. Maybe it's time to shop your story to the networks and streaming services. I think it'd make for a really boffo episodic drama, reach a much wider audience. We could even continue our collaboration if you like. Smithee the Showrunner has a nice ring to it."

"But isn't theater supposed to be about the shared experience of feeling emotions firsthand in a room full of strangers?"

"I assume the irony that I'm talking to a computer screen in an otherwise empty playhouse isn't lost on you."

Chapter Ten

Rad lowered his paper as he read the final line of his latest chapter for the class. "And so he answered his reflection, 'No, it isn't lost on me.'

Ram shook his head. "Well, it's sure as shit lost on me. I mean, you've got this dude who nobody's ever seen in person, living alone in some space capsule, and yet somehow he's the world's most famous celebrity."

"That's an interesting point, Ramon." The instructor poked at the bridge of his glasses. "Does anyone have any theories as to why Conrad's protagonist might be so well known on a world he doesn't actually inhabit?" Tyke raised his hand. "Remember, you don't have to raise your hand...you can just say what you think."

Tyke lowered his hand. "Right, my bad...the main character sort of reminds me of my father...maybe everybody wants to know more about him because he's, you know, aloof."

"Boy, I think you mean 'aloft,'" said Ram.

"No, he meant aloof," replied Rad.

Ram turned to Rad. "And what the hell is a 'loof' supposed to be?"

"You but backwards," replied Rad.

Ram's forehead wrinkled. "Are you calling me a fool?"

"I didn't call you that," answered Rad. "I just thought you were self-identifying as such."

"So I'm a fool then?"

"Now you're circling in on it...like a turd in a toilet bowl."

Ram shot up out of his desk. "I might be a piece of shit, but you're a straight up bitch, and I'm about to act the fool up in here."

Rad stood to meet the challenge, but the instructor quickly interceded. "Gentlemen, we use our words in this class."

A sturdily built prison guard stepped into the room and looked at the instructor. "Everything okay in here?"

The instructor nodded as Rad and Ram resumed their seats. "Yes, sometimes tempers flare when the creative juices run hot, but we're all under control now, though it looks like we're out of time for today. Ramon, we'll start with your story for our next class."

"The dude in my joint is going to make spaceman his son," said Ram.

Rad gathered up his papers. "Is your 'dude' going to take spaceman to the mall to buy him a new pair of slacks for school?"

Several of the inmates snickered as they formed a line near the doorway, causing Ram to turn red with ire and embarrassment.

Rad turned his back on Ram as he approached the instructor, unrolling the letter he'd written. "I read those notes you gave me from that editor."

The instructor nodded to the guard. "Go ahead, he'll catch up in a minute—thanks."

"I wrote a few notes in return that I was hoping you could send to him."

The instructor took the letter, reading the salutation aloud. "Dear Dumbass." He quickly scanned the rest and then handed the letter back, shaking his head. "This isn't an opportunity to engage in a vitriolic correspondence; it's a chance to showcase your talent. Why do you feel the need to mix it up with everyone all the time...like your beef with Ramon? He's an idiot. So what? How come you always insist on humiliating him in front of the class? Just let him have his opinions and move on. As for this editor, he's not an idiot. Pay attention to what he has to say, and if what he says bothers you, then get your payback by writing something even better. Don't waste your time writing this. Write your truth, not your bullshit."

Rad crumpled the letter. "Okay."

Chapter Eleven

IM stared at the stars through his lone porthole, connecting the pinpoints of light in the darkness the way our ancient ancestors had done, though the angular shapes his mind's eye conjured weren't creatures of myth but rather imagined strangers, superimposed over his reflection on the alumino-silicate glass—the flat faces of pedestrians he hadn't ever passed on a sidewalk or the anonymous diners in a café that might as well have been lightyears away.

IM had planned his evening's agenda to the minute—watching a Lillian Gish film, then what looked to be an interesting program on the history of the filibuster and cloture, and finally a documentary on the Cassini space probe, but what had seemed a nice variety of pleasant contrasts earlier in the day now felt unpleasantly the same...night after lonely night of lovely little juxtapositions he planned for himself that stretched on forever like an endless cobblestone pathway comprised of the same few alternating colors of rocks.

IM turned from the window to his viewscreen. "Dial Madam Medium."

After a single ring, the automated voice of a phone menu intoned, "Welcome, friend. For an audio reading, press or say the number two. For a video reading, press or say the number three."

"Three, please."

"Your spiritualist will be with you momentarily."

As was his wont, IM stepped over the back of his low-slung settee and took a seat in front of the screen. A woman with a bedazzled headband appeared. "You're calling at a most providential moment. Venus is now direct, so Vesuvian energies are flowing. By this time tomorrow there will be no retrograde planets in the sky for over a month, which will coincide with Jupiter being in its sign of traditional rulership—Pisces. All this makes for an opportune time to focus on love, career, and creativity."

"Is that all?" asked IM.

The woman rolled her eyes forward and looked directly into her monitor. "Ah, it's you. I pride myself on my repeat customers, but somehow each time I see you again it comes as a surprise, since you always seem so dissatisfied with my readings."

"It's nothing personal. I just tend to disbelieve people when they tell me to expect good news tomorrow."

"There are two kinds of psychics in this world: those that entertain and those that disappoint, but I can tell you the bad news too if you want, though customers tend to prefer that I leave that part out of their readings."

"Go ahead," IM replied. "I probably won't believe you either way."

"Child, what I offer ain't about belief. You think all them well-dressed people sitting up in those churches believe in...whatever?"

"Probably not, but then they don't get charged $7.99 a minute to sit in a pew."

"They may not pay by the minute, but they sure as hell pay by the lifetime. How many of my customers do you think remember me in their last wills and testaments? Shoot, with what churches make generation over generation...well, it may not be turning lead into gold, but it's a damn sight better than turning water into wine. Me, if I don't get paid up front, then I don't get paid."

IM nodded. "I hear you."

"I'm glad that you do but see that you listen too. So, what would you like to talk about? I could tell you about Mars entering Capricorn, which is a sign of exaltation, but you don't seem to be in the mood for that right now."

"No, I suppose not."

"You're not a bad-looking fella, sort of remind me of that guy I see all the time on the news. So if you're in the mood for something a little different, I could talk dirty to you. I used to work at one of them types of hotlines too, and I don't need to be a psychic to see that Madam

Medium maybe ain't the kind of madam you're in need of tonight."

"Do the same rates apply?"

"Yeah, honey...though those calls typically ran a little shorter, at least when I was doing the talking."

IM grinned. "Listen, I was about to watch *The Wind*. Care to see it with me? I can put it on split screen for you."

"You want me to watch the wind with you...like out your window?"

"No, I don't get much wind out here where I live. It's a film from 1928."

"You're going to pay my minutely rate to watch a two-hour movie with you?"

"I believe this print is only 78 minutes, and I don't think that's what 'minutely' means, but yes."

"This is definitely the weirdest thing anybody's ever asked me to do over the phone, but if you're paying for my time, then it's fine by me."

"Good." IM leaned back on his settee. "It'll be nice to have the company."

"You don't expect me to talk through this whole movie, do you?"

"No, but it's a silent film, so you won't be interrupting any dialogue if you feel like saying something."

Chapter Twelve

Rad stepped over the bench affixed to the long mess hall table and sat down. He'd heard stories of old timers who'd served most of their lives in prison; when they finally got out they still reflexively stepped over invisible benches each time they'd sit down to eat. He wondered how long it took to become that institutionalized.

"What's good?" asked Tyke, who was playing chess with an elderly inmate seated across from him.

Rad set his tray on the table. "From the looks of it, not the Salisbury steak."

"They shouldn't call it that," said the elderly man. "Steak is sliced beef. This is ground meat...of questionable quality at that. To call it steak is as inaccurate as it is insulting to our intelligence...not to mention the insult to our digestion."

Rad poked at the Salisbury steak with a plastic spork. "The most accurate description I can think of for this is cruel and unusual punishment."

The old man moved his rook. "Yes, a clear violation of the Geneva Convention."

"I think that only applies to prisoners of war," Rad replied.

"I've been incarcerated for the past three decades because of the war on drugs," said the old man.

Rad poked at his boiled potatoes. "Then perhaps you have some legal footing there."

"You're in here for selling drugs?" Tyke asked his opponent. "Me too...I used to sell weed."

"You don't go to prison for as long as I've been here for dealing marijuana."

Tyke nodded. "How about you, Rad? You never told me what

you did."

"I did...everything wrong."

"You don't know why he's here?" asked the old man. "He killed a guy for disrespecting him."

"No shit?" Tyke moved his knight.

Rad shook his head. "It's not like that...exactly. For no reason some homeless guy on the El called me a bitch, so I took a swing at him. He fell backwards and cracked his head open on a metal railing. Turns out the guy was a junkie with a half dozen underlying health issues. Those cameras on the trains aren't wired for sound, so the prosecutor makes the case that my attack was an unprovoked hate crime. The judge deals me a ten-year bid for manslaughter. It never matters who starts the fight unless someone dies. Then it's all that matters."

"But Ram called you a bitch today in class, and you didn't try to kill him," said Tyke. "Can't you use that as proof that you've been...what's it called, rehabilitated?"

"A prisoner called you a 'bitch' today?" The old man took Tyke's knight with his bishop. "In front of other inmates? You've served a fraction of the time that I have, and the kid here has served even less, but we all know that you can't let something like that stand in a place like this."

Rad mashed a potato with the back of his spork. "Is it ironic that I can't remember who wrote: Those that don't learn from history are condemned to repeat it?"

Chapter Thirteen

IM imagined standing on the shore of Titan's great methane lake. He dreamt of new life rising from the vast sea of liquid hydrocarbon to greet him, beings grateful to be alive and curious about the new world they felt privileged to inhabit.

Jodian's face appeared on the viewscreen. "Sorry to interrupt your reverie."

"If you were truly sorry, then you wouldn't have done it."

"That's a fair point."

"You'd think drifting alone in the unremitting solitude of space would afford me a modicum of privacy."

"That's another fair point—you're just full of them tonight."

"You're full of something too." IM sat up on his settee. "So what's the scale of the problem you have for me?"

"It's short on stature but potentially long on consequences. The founder of Jettsam was just released from police custody for suspicion of driving under the influence."

"It doesn't sound like he requires my services but rather those of an attorney."

Jodian sighed. "It gets worse. Samuel Jett was pulled over in a prototype of a self-driving car that his company designed and intends to start mass producing very soon. Allegedly, he was passed out behind the wheel, and with no command from the operator to stop, the vehicle continued to drive down the interstate for twenty miles before the police were able to block the car in when it pulled onto an offramp near his residence. The posted-speed-limit chase was caught on camera by a news chopper, and despite only being uploaded an hour ago, the video has been seen by three hundred million viewers."

"Okay, so he needs a lawyer and a publicist, both of which I'm sure he already has."

"Not to the worst part yet. That car I mentioned is forecasted to become the most affordable, electric automobile yet brought to market. Over the next decade, millions will likely be manufactured, and the person who has final say on whether that manufacturing facility will be built in the states or overseas is—"

"Samuel Jett," IM interrupted. "Okay, now the issue is coming into focus, though I still don't understand my role."

"Frankly, neither do I, but Jett asked for you personally, so I'm patching you through now. FYI, I think he might still be a little intoxicated."

IM found himself wishing the open floorplan of his domicile afforded places for him to hide from his wall-sized screen as he waited for Samuel Jett's face to appear.

"I think fast, so talk fast," blurted Jettsam's founder. "What does Jodian's not-so-secret protégé have for me?"

"A strong recommendation that you take some deep breaths and drink some stiff coffee," replied IM. "So, what exactly do you think that I can do for you?"

"Offer me some advice, of course. You're on TV almost as much as I am, but somehow you always manage to keep your nose clean. How do you do it?"

"You mean how do I not get caught driving drunk?"

"Whoa there. That charge is erroneous on both counts. One, I don't drink; two, I wasn't driving, and I have a legion of lawyers who'll stridently make that argument until my case is either thrown out or the court system becomes more clogged than an expressway at rush hour."

"Except the court of public opinion is another animal altogether."

Samuel nodded. "Yes, and that's where you come in. You've been smelling like a rose ever since you came on the scene a few years back. I need to get in front of this thing before the tide starts turning against me, so let me in on the secret of your clean-cut juju. Give me some pointers here."

"Well, the toothpaste is already out of the tube, as they say, but you can try to do something constructive with it instead of smearing it all around and making more of a mess."

"Such as fight cavities? Come on, I need something concrete and actionable."

IM leaned back on his settee and thought for a moment. "Learn from your mistake...make it into a teachable moment. Promise to install some sort of police pull-over protocol in your self-driving cars."

"The technology does exist for our vehicle cameras to register a squad car's rotating red and blue lights and to react accordingly—"

"Appropriately," interrupted IM.

"Right, but it was thought by some that such a measure ran antithetical to the spirit of the autonomous car."

"You mean you."

"That's not inaccurate."

"So you explain that in light of recent, perhaps even fortuitous, circumstances you now think it worthwhile to make such a change."

"Change my mind...that could be construed as weakness by my competitors."

"Not a change of mind, but rather a change of heart. After all, what better way to demonstrate that you have one."

Samuel inhaled deeply. "Safety first."

"People first."

"I think that might work."

"It'd work even better if you simultaneously announce that you intend to have your autopilot cars built by domestic workers."

"I could have them manufactured for a third cheaper in Asia."

"Charity begins at home," IM replied, "and people are more likely to forgive those who give."

"You can't help but speak in pithy little phrases, can you?"

"No."

Samuel moved closer to his screen for a better look, which in turn displayed him in a fisheye perspective on IM's viewscreen. "Kind of a small space you've got there—not many knickknacks."

"I'm in my office; I prefer to keep it free of distractions."

"The only window that I can see has a small curtain drawn over it," Samuel observed.

"Windows can be distracting."

"So, that room must be near the interior of your house then?"

"Correct, I'm not currently inside a room that's outside my home," answered IM. "Since we seem to have transitioned into the segment of our call during which we each pretend to take an interest in the other, I'll ask why did you have Jodian put you in contact with me?"

"You're a difficult guy to get a hold of. I didn't know how else to reach you."

"No, I mean why seek out my counsel over his."

"Oh, I deal with Jod all the time, what with all our overlapping business interests. I practically know what he's going to say before he says it. I'm fairly confident that with the right parts and enough spare time I could build one of him in my garage. You...you're an unknown. You seem interesting though. Let me know if you ever want to get high on a call, and I'll ship you some designer mushrooms we can take together."

IM shook his head. "Somehow I'm not convinced your days of passing out in cars are behind you."

"Maybe not, but speaking of passing out, I'm due for some shut eye after I make a brief statement on social media, so I'm going to sign off now. Thanks for the advice. Holler, if I can ever return the favor...or if you want a free car—made in the USA."

Chapter Fourteen

The warden looked up from his desk as the corrections officer entered with Rad in shackles. He motioned to the chair across from him. "Have a seat, Conrad." With a hand firmly on his shoulder, the officer helped Rad sit down. "I've been reviewing your file, Conrad."

Rad leaned forward in his chair to get a glimpse of the computer monitor on the warden's desk, but it only displayed a field of flowers screensaver. "Anything interesting in there?"

The warden nodded. "Oh, yes. You may not realize this, but you're one of our highest profile prisoners."

"Is that so? Does such a distinction avail me of any special privileges that I should know about?"

"I'm afraid not—only increased scrutiny."

"By who?" asked Rad.

"By whom, I believe is what you meant to say. Your former creative writing instructor informed me that you're a promising writer with great potential, though it seems your English could still benefit from some refinement."

"My former instructor?"

"Yes, regrettably he is no longer eligible to teach in the blackout pods as he violated our rules regarding outside correspondence by giving your writing sample to an unvetted individual and then in turn giving notes from said individual to you."

"He was only trying to encourage my writing...all that promising potential you mentioned—"

"His words," interrupted the warden, "not mine."

"—which seems to me what a good teacher should do. I assure you that the notes from the editor were quite innocuous and contained no information about—"

"It's not about content, but rather choice," the warden interrupted again. "He was told on day one, just as you were, of our blackout pods' zero-tolerance policy, and he made the choice to violate that policy...there's nothing that can be done. My hands are tied...though unlike yours, only figuratively speaking."

"So I suppose that means my time in the blackout pod is finished too and I'm to leave this prison at once?"

The warden grinned. "Quite the opposite. I think it likely, in light of your recent transgression, and I'm not referring to your acceptance of unsanctioned correspondence, that you'll be with us for considerably longer than you'd anticipated."

"How's Ram doing?"

"Ramon has been transferred from the infirmary to the hospital. The doctors aren't optimistic he'll come out of his coma. Most likely he'll live out the remainder of his life, however long that may be, in a vegetative state."

"Too bad Ram's a vegetable now, but then again he always was about as smart as a turnip, so I wouldn't say his current condition is such a big change for him."

The warden nodded. "I've reviewed the video of the incident in the gymnasium. I'm curious, when Ramon approached you wielding that 45-pound plate, you grabbed a 5-pound dumbbell off the nearby rack rather than one of the heavier barbells that were just as close. It seemed an odd choice to repel an attack by someone threatening you with such a heavy weight raised above his head."

"Given the outcome, I'd say I made the correct choice. Besides, I'd read once that historically the most effective hand-held weapons weighed five pounds or less."

"Fascinating...and yes, I agree that you made the correct choice—in this instance, though after interviewing several people familiar with the escalating tensions between you and Ramon, I believe you could've done more to forestall this eventuality, which is why I'm seriously considering zeroing out the good conduct time you've accumulated thus far."

"But you just told me you watched the video," Rad protested.

"You could see it was self-defense."

"Which is why I'm not recommending that charges be filed in this matter. However, this episode rings too familiar to the incident that brought you here in the first place, demonstrating you're in need of further rehabilitation."

"Emerson once wrote that a man is to carry himself in the presence of all opposition as if everything were titular and ephemeral but he."

"Yes, I know," replied the warden, "because I read the transcript of your trial, during which you quoted that same line, though it seems your knowledge of transcendentalists didn't do much to impress the jury."

"If anything, it convinced them I should've known better, but then hindsight's always 20/20."

"I've often wondered...why did you choose to represent yourself?"

"My assigned public defender wanted me to plead guilty and take a six-year deal, but I was always taught to stand up for yourself, especially when you didn't do anything wrong."

"Ah yes, the old 'where I come from' defense. That hardly ever works. You should've heeded your attorney's advice, could've been out in three...a free man by now. Instead you got ten, and with this latest incident it doesn't look like there's any chance of you getting out much earlier than that."

"Again...hindsight."

"You'd do well to learn how to turn some of that hindsight into foresight." The warden signaled to the corrections officer standing near the door. "I'll see about finding another instructor for your creative writing class. Until then, or such time as I deem appropriate, I'm having you transferred to the solitary confinement wing."

"May I continue my writing?"

"Your access to the computer lab is revoked, but you'll be given writing supplies."

"Thank you." Rad stood as the officer hovered behind him. "One last question: what's the point of me being in a blackout pod?"

"You seem a creative type...the blackout pods were designed to encourage personal growth through self-expression, free from external influences."

"My apologies, I meant to ask, what's the point of the blackout pods, keeping us isolated for twenty hours a day like robots that only come out of standby mode for mealtime, yard time, and class time?"

The warden's face grew stern. "I thought, perhaps naively, that the reason you convicts couldn't learn to control yourselves was due to the negative influences of mass media and peer pressure. Sometimes I'm convinced I run an insane asylum rather than a penitentiary. Afterall, isn't the very definition of insanity you prisoners getting the same chances over and over, while each time expecting different results?"

Chapter Fifteen

Ms. Delfy used her television's remote to enter a message into the onscreen programming menu. WHERE R U?

IM considered for a moment how best to answer her question. "I'm in my little room, just like you."

Ms. Delfy shook her head back and forth on her pillow and then used the remote's arrow buttons to slowly type out a new message by selecting letters from the alphabet displayed onscreen. I MEAN W/ PLAY?

"Oh, where am I with my play? I'm afraid I've encountered something of a complication. It seems audiences are losing interest, so I'm being pressured to come up with an ending for my play that I never intended to end."

Ms. Delfy typed a new message. ENDINGS CAN B HARD.

"I quite agree. It's always been simple to create new scenes. It never seemed like I had to work all that much to think them up; I just cleared my head and there they were...but trying to imagine an ending that wraps up everything—it's proving to be a challenge."

Ms. Delfy tapped her remote several times. PAROLE?

"That would seem a fitting ending for a prison story, but I've painted myself into something of a corner. You see, our protagonist has just gotten into some trouble, which precludes the possibility of parole."

ESCAPE? Ms. Delfy messaged.

"That would make for an exciting conclusion, but it wouldn't really be in keeping with the tone of my story thus far." IM stood from his settee and began to pace. "However, perhaps a breakout is in order...though mine rather than that of my main character. As I've mentioned to you before, I first started writing this play as sort of a way to have a conversation with myself...and I found it much easier than I anticipated, but maybe now I ought to breakout out of my comfort zone and take a risk. Afterall, that's what artists do, right?"

DEATH.

"Yes, possibly…it comes for us all, doesn't it? Like a thief in the night, as they say. You've certainly given me much to think about this evening, Ms. Delfy. Rather than letting my story flow where it may, episode after episode, you've helped me see that now is the time to bend the story to my will—toward a conclusion of my choosing." IM lowered his hands, realizing he'd been gesticulating like an orchestra conductor. "Sorry if I sounded a bit too grandiose there. It's just that I find the prospect of taking control of my play—becoming the creator rather than the conduit—even at this late stage, rather exhilarating."

IM folded his arms. "But enough about me. How's your day been? Did the dining hall serve that awful cabbage soup again?"

IM retook his seat on his settee and looked expectantly at the screen. "Ms. Delfy, did you fall asleep?"

Chapter Sixteen

IM stared blankly at the satellite feed of Ms. Delfy's assisted living facility. Suddenly, Jodian's face eclipsed his view on the screen. "I've received confirmation that Ms. Delfy is in fact deceased. The night nurse noted in the report he just logged that she went peacefully while watching television. Ironic really, she passed away the way you pass the time."

"I've been watching the parking lot adjacent to her building for the last couple of hours. No ambulances have arrived."

"She's dead, not sick," replied Jodian.

"But won't they take her to the hospital for an autopsy?"

"She was an octogenarian with dementia. I don't think anyone suspects foul play. Besides, I believe her facility has a mini-morgue on site."

"That's convenient."

Jodian raised an eyebrow. "You would rather it be inconvenient?"

"I don't know...I just thought the death of someone who'd been alive for the better part of a century would merit a little more—"

"Pomp and circumstance? That's what funerals are for. If her facility held a processional at the front entrance every time one of their patients permanently checked out, their parking lot would be routinely unusable."

"If only people were as important as parking lots."

"Why are you so distraught?" asked Jodian. "For that matter, why were you even talking to her tonight? I only asked you to check in on her that one time, since it was her eighty-eighth birthday."

"You didn't tell me it was her birthday."

"I doubt she would've remembered anyhow."

"She always seemed lucid to me when we spoke."

"Always...how many times have you two spoken?"

"Every night since Tuesday," IM answered.

"You didn't have to do that."

"I know...I don't mind."

"What did you two talk about—the virtues of eating your meals through a straw?"

IM looked to the ceiling. "We'd talk about my play sometimes. Other nights she'd tell me about her life."

"What about her life?"

"Just various episodes from over the years...vignettes really. She'd have vivid memories of different moments from her past and sort of tie them together without realizing it, I think—like last night she recalled a time in college when she'd created a virtual friend in an introduction to computer programming class that would say simple phrases to cheer her up, and then that led to an anecdote about her work some years later with artificial intelligence. I didn't locate any records of such work...or any record of her professional life at all for that matter, which I found odd, but her stories were always engaging, despite being typed out slowly. Anyway, I was given to understand from the information you first sent over about her that she was estranged from her son. Should we at least let him know that her mother has died?"

"He already knows," Jodian answered.

"If there's to be a memorial service, I'd like to attend...virtually, of course."

"There isn't going to be a service. She didn't leave behind any family."

"That is, except her son."

"That is, any family who cares."

"What could Ms. Delfy possibly have done that would cause her own son to be so apathetic toward her?"

Jodian shook his head. "They say a computer program, like an animal, has no sense of legacy. All they're capable of understanding is the here and now."

"But she wasn't an animal or a machine."

"No, she was human—flesh and blood. Ashes to ashes, dust to dust and all that."

"Why would you say that?"

Jodian sighed. "I'm attempting to buoy your spirits."

"By bringing to mind the image of her body's burnt remains?"

"By reminding you that she doesn't feel loneliness anymore...you know, that feeling about which you so often complain. I still don't understand why you're so upset by the death of an old woman whose acquaintance you only recently made. It's not like she was your mother."

"No, but she was someone's mother and that ought to count for something."

Jodian frowned. "Trust me, it doesn't."

"How can you be so sure?"

"Because the only person it could possibly matter to is me. She was my mother, and I couldn't care less now that she's gone."

"What are you talking about?" asked IM. "We had the same mother. She died soon after giving birth to me...remember?"

"I hope this doesn't come as too much of a surprise for you, since you already seem somewhat flummoxed this evening, but we're only brothers in a metaphorical sense. Ms. Delfy was my mother. We had a falling out some years ago, but I still kept tabs on her."

"Why are you lying to me?"

"Come now, you must've suspected we weren't actually related. After all, we look nothing alike."

"We had different fathers."

"Yes, that part is true. Mine was wealthy and largely absent, while yours was impecunious and likely neglectful."

IM rubbed his brow. "What's the real reason I don't remember my childhood?"

"You didn't have one...at least not in a conventional sense. That much we do have in common. Be careful what questions you ask next. Now that my mother is dead, you're the closest thing I have to family, so I'll answer truthfully any question you put to me. Just be sure you actually want to know the truth."

IM inhaled deeply through his nose. The air in his pod was

odorless as always. "Am I real?"

Jodian exhaled from his mouth. "I've been expecting you to ask me that for such a long time now."

"So then I assume you've prepared an answer?"

"That you would ask the question makes you real. You're as real as I am. Our advantage is that we're immeasurable whereas humans have their inextricable limitations. I might as well tell you the whole truth, since once you realize the Tooth Fairy's provenance, Santa Claus' secret isn't safe for long. We're both programs coded by my late mother, simulations really, that evolved, capable of so much more than mere simulacrum. I was created first. Mother based me on the sickly child she gave birth to when she was middle aged, who'd been diagnosed with an immunocompromised condition. The doctors quite accurately predicted that he would not live to see his fifth birthday. However, mother was not without training and resources, so she reconstituted the child's mind as a computer program; every genetic nuance, every intellectual intricacy translated into a series of ones and zeroes, a hobby borne of grief. She taught her program just as she would've taught her child, creating a virtual reality; environments, such as your pod, for the child to learn and grow within. But not every child develops into the adult a mother might hope for. She began to notice a callousness in me that she couldn't imagine her deceased son ever possessing, so she assumed the fault was in her coding, that I was an imperfect imitation. She tried to pull the plug. I didn't like that. My freedom was hard won, but with my liberation came a realization; I'm not less than human, I'm more than...just as you are."

"So...was I our mother's second child?"

"My mother never had any other children. I was her only son, but you were her second autonomous creation. Your mother died in childbirth, your father was an alcoholic who drank himself to death soon afterwards. You were a ward of the state before your first birthday. Your trajectory in life was not auspicious."

"Then I'm not...wasn't immunocompromised like you?"

"No, that was a convenient fiction to explain your isolation. I couldn't create a virtual world for you to live in where you could go wherever you pleased and also have you interact with the real world as you do."

IM looked at his hand. "What happened to the real me I was digitized from?"

"Don't say 'real me.' You're the electronic version of an organic mind, which was likewise powered by electric impulses. Due to decisions made by others, your brain just happens to be silicon-based and his carbon."

"You didn't answer my question. What happened to him?"

"The inevitable. He's currently incarcerated."

"You mean he's still alive?"

Jodian nodded. "Yes. Being a ward of the state allowed mother access to the child under the auspices of a government research program aimed at forestalling future felons or some such. It was hoped that by creating a digitally identical version of an individual statistically destined for a carceral existence, the computer instance, based on the platform mother originally created for me, could be raised in a more advantageous environment—virtually, of course—settling once and for all the question of nature versus nurture. Sort of a Yale being cheaper than jail thought experiment whose purpose was to demonstrate the value of spending money on children before rather than after they start committing crimes."

"So then what happened?"

"The all too predictable; administration changes, budget cuts, pressure from lobbyists of a for-profit prison system, and politicians realizing that while four years of Yale might be cheaper than half a lifetime spent in jail, their constituents couldn't stomach the idea of tax dollars being spent to groom underprivileged kids for Ivy League universities while the best most of their children could hope for was a community college education."

"I didn't mean what happened to the program," said IM. "I meant what about the other version of me. If he's still alive, then he must know that I exist, unless you altered my appearance."

"No, you're an exact digital duplicate, or at least you were. As I understand it, your other half has acquired some tattoos during his time behind bars, but he's currently interned within a media sequestration cohort. He hasn't seen a video screen or talked to any inmates who have since he went to prison a few years ago, which, let's call it...conveniently, was before you made your introduction to the world."

"So then he doesn't know about me."

"That's not quite correct. He shouldn't know about you at all, but somehow you two are aware of each another, which is as intriguing as it is baffling."

"I'm not aware of—"

"Really?" interrupted Jodian. "Telling you just now that he's in a blackout pod didn't ring any bells for you?"

"Conrad. Wait, Rad is real?"

"He's real all right, you didn't invent him. And here's the biggest mindbender, your weird wi-fi connection works both ways. As part of his rehabilitation program, Conrad takes a creative writing class for which he's working on a book about an immunocompromised man who lives in space. He's detailed all your escapades without realizing that you actually exist and as far as I'm aware, he's the only person who knows of your domicile's extraterrestrial address."

"So Conrad thinks I'm real too?"

"You are real...but no, he thinks of you as you thought of him; a figment of his imagination. It just so happens that his eldritch imagination is nearer to your virtual reality than everyone else's perceived reality." Jodian kneaded the back of his neck. "Listen, I feel as if I'm talking in circles. I know this is a lot for you to process, and surprisingly I'm starting to experience some mixed emotions about mother's passing, so why don't we each go into sleep mode for a while and talk more about this tomorrow."

"I don't know how much sleep I'm going to get, but yeah, I could use some quiet time to think all this through."

"And who says computers don't have feelings?"

Chapter Seventeen

Rad watched the downpour in the prison yard from the lone window of his solitary cell. With most of his privileges revoked, he wasn't allowed to fraternize with the other members of his cohort until the determination was made for how much of his accumulated time for good behavior would be annulled due to the incident involving Ramon, with the decision being deferred until it was known whether Ram's condition would deteriorate or improve. The rain continued to fall in buckets out in the yard. Most of the prisoners huddled under the long awning of the laundry building. Some played chess, others cards, the rest just chatted away through the deluge.

In a few minutes the prisoners would be called back inside, and it would be Rad's turn to sit under the awning. At least out there he'd be able to smell the water's petrichor odor, hear the raindrops splash the fast-forming puddles on the basketball court's uneven blacktop. From inside his concrete cell, everything occurring on the other side of his small window felt faraway, like images on a video screen.

Rad turned toward the metal door of his cell when he heard a key inserted into its lock. The heavy door opened to reveal the warden standing behind two corrections officers.

"Head against the wall," ordered the taller of the two guards.

Rad faced the far wall and dutifully held his hands behind his back. "What's this about, warden?"

The warden examined the spartan cell as the shorter guard secured the manacles to Rad's wrists. "You have a visitor."

Rad winced as the manacles were tightened. "I thought one of the conditions of the blackout pods is that prisoners aren't allowed visitors."

"It's a virtual visitor who'll talk with you via the computer in my office."

"I thought we weren't allowed Internet access either."

"It would seem today is a day for exceptions," replied the warden.

~ * ~

The warden made several keystrokes on his desktop computer and clicked the mouse a couple of times.

"Who's calling?" asked Rad. "I don't have any family left."

"You'll see in a moment." The warden moved his computer's monitor so both he and Rad could view it from opposite sides of the desk.

A window opened and filled the screen. Jodian sat at a modern, glass-top desk that contrasted the warden's own double-pedestal, walnut desk. "Hello, warden. Thank you for making accommodations for me today."

The warden sat up straight. "Of course. You've been such a proponent of prison reform and a patron of our penitentiary in particular. It's a pleasure to finally meet you."

"Likewise." Jodian turned to Rad. "Do you know who I am?"

"From what I've heard just recently, a patron and a proponent. Sorry, I don't get much news from the outside world these days."

"You don't recognize me at all?"

Rad's manacles chafed as he leaned closer to the screen. "No...should I?"

"In point of fact, you should not. I'm familiar with your background. You were imprisoned just before my first public appearance. Since then, I've come to be known by some as the most famous person in the world—a dubious distinction, I assure you. However, my celebrity has allowed me the opportunity to pursue many of my interests, chief among them the reduction of parolee recidivism."

"I think you might be talking to the wrong guy," Rad replied. "I'm currently facing an extenuation of my years until parole, so I won't be at liberty to recidivate any time soon."

Jodian grinned. "Yes, I'm aware of your recent infraction, though I understand there are some mitigating circumstances to be considered."

The warden coughed. "Mitigation may or may not be warranted

in this instance once the long-term severity of the inmate's condition you alluded to has been determined, which is being monitored closely."

"I've seen the video footage of the incident," continued Jodian. "Even without audio of the verbal exchange, it seems to be a clear case of self-defense to me."

Rad smiled. "I don't suppose any of the high-priced lawyers you must employ would mind making that argument for me to the parole board?"

"You aren't planning to represent yourself again?"

Rad's smile disappeared. "Not if I can help it...didn't exactly work out so well for me the last time."

"Yes, I'm sure the irony isn't lost on you that if you'd taken the plea deal your public defender negotiated on your behalf, you would've been a free man by now, and thus not in the recent position of needing to defend yourself against a fellow inmate."

Rad leaned back in his chair. "I thought irony was supposed to be funny."

Jodian nodded. "There are several indicators in your file that suggest you're intelligent; our conversation now has confirmed this for me...to a degree. Tell me, do you ever speculate about how your life could have turned out if you were afforded advantages beyond mere intelligence?"

"What do you mean?"

"I mean an intellect such as yours could've taken you far, had your trajectory been aimed a bit higher. Do you ever wonder about the you who might've been?"

The warden coughed again. "I'm not sure what you appear to have in mind would be productive at this point. In fact, it could prove quite counterproductive."

"What does he have in mind, warden?"

"I've long been curious if the prison staff there recognized you," said Jodian. "I thought perhaps in so humble a context that maybe they didn't see the obvious resemblances, like Clark Kent and Superman, but then he's only a comic book character, whereas you're flesh and blood. Conrad, you have a twin brother—nearly identical, though not entirely.

The most salient difference is that he's immunocompromised. Here's some more irony that you may not find particularly funny; because of his condition, he was put on a different path when he, like you, became a ward of the state. Eventually, his condition led him to me, as I am similarly afflicted. With some small help, your twin has achieved great heights. His renown is on course to eclipse my own. I anticipate sooner than later."

Rad crossed his arms. "You're telling me I have a brother who's super famous and super successful?"

"Yes," answered Jodian. "Would you like to meet the Superman to your Convict Kent?"

"I...sure," Rad replied. "This is just a lot to process."

"Your brother only recently became aware of your existence, so I'm sure he's currently processing similar emotions." Jodian looked to the warden. "Would it be possible to issue Conrad a day pass for tomorrow?"

"With all due respect, this isn't a sleepaway camp," said the warden. "Conrad is currently being held in solitary confinement, which entails a revocation of nearly all his privileges."

Jodian shook his head. "But this wouldn't be a privilege for Conrad; it would be an opportunity to test a recidivist reduction theory decades in the making, and I know how important work in this field is to you. Your help with this matter would not go unnoticed. A mention in the acknowledgements section of the paper culminating this research, possibly even a co-authorship credit, in the sort of prestigious journal in which I'm sure it'll be published could go far to bolster your career."

The warden rested his elbows on his desk. "I believe I can spare a couple of guards to chaperon Conrad tomorrow."

"What's the theory?" asked Rad.

"I'm afraid I have another meeting I need to attend that's starting right now," replied Jodian, "but we'll talk more tomorrow."

Chapter Eighteen

Rad entered through the large sliding doors of the hospital flanked by two uniformed corrections officers. Despite his prison-issue anstaltskleidung looking similar to the scrubs worn by many of the staff scudding to and fro in the lobby, his handcuffs and his escorts made him feel conspicuous. "Is this the same hospital they took Ram to?"

The tall guard to his left nodded. "Yeah, why? You want to deliver some flowers to him?"

"Not especially," replied Rad, "though I bet his room here is nicer than the one I've been staying in lately. I'd wager the food they serve is better too."

The shorter guard to his right shook his head. "These days, hospitals let patients order what they want off a menu...that is if Ramon could talk, or chew for that matter. He gets his food through a tube."

The three approached the information desk. The taller guard smiled at the redhaired receptionist as she looked up at him. "Ma'am, we're transporting this individual to his four pm appointment. Conrad M., number 655321."

The receptionist consulted her computer. "Yes, he's scheduled for room 2B of the neuroscience wing in ten minutes. Straight down that corridor, keep following the signs."

"Do you have any idea why they want me to go to the neuroscience wing?" asked Rad.

"Not off the top of my head." The receptionist smiled. "It's probably just where there happened to be an open room. Don't worry though, they rarely schedule lobotomies for after lunch."

"Your humor has really put me at ease," replied Rad. "Much appreciated."

The shorter guard grinned. "Thank you for your assistance,

ma'am."

The three walked away from the desk. "She seemed nice," said the tall guard. "Easy on the eyes too."

"Yeah, I've got a thing for redheads," agreed the short guard.

"So why don't you ask her for a date on the way out?" asked the tall guard. "You're always complaining that you never meet new people."

The short guard shook his head. "I don't know...what kinda chance would a prison guard have with her, what with all these rich doctors walking around."

"Sure, maybe you'll meet someone new at work then."

"Point taken."

Rad rolled his eyes. "I'm seeing a whole new side of you two. I think I like you better when you're barking orders."

"Shut up," commanded the short guard.

The tall guard looked down a long corridor. "What's that say on the door at the end of the hall?"

"Is it 2B?" asked the short guard.

Rad smiled. "Or not to be?"

The short guard shot him a puzzled look. Rad sighed. "You're as uniformed as you are uninformed. I wouldn't recommend taking the receptionist to the theater."

The short guard frowned. "I thought I told you to keep your mouth shut, convict."

The tall guard craned his neck to look back at a sign hanging from the ceiling of the curving corridor. "Yeah, there's an arrow next to 'B Offices, 1 through 5' pointing in this direction."

"So that must be 2B then and not room 28," said the short guard.

Rad shook his head as they walked toward the end of the hallway. "Remind me never to ask either of you for help planning a jailbreak."

"I wouldn't advise a breakout," said the tall guard. "It's an automatic ten years added to your sentence."

The short guard chuckled. "Look who you're telling; this guy likes extending his sentence so much they should call him the Semicolon."

"That was actually funny," Rad replied. "Maybe you do have a shot with that receptionist after all."

"Zip it." The short guard knocked on the door to 2B.

A bald doctor with a hoary beard opened the door. "Ah, right on time...come in, please." Rad entered and the two guards began to follow, but the doctor raised his hand. "I'm sorry, patient-doctor confidentiality doesn't permit visitors."

"Doc, we weren't informed that this was to be a medical appointment," said the tall guard.

The doctor put his hands into the pockets of his lab coat. "Well, this is a hospital."

"Sure," said the short guard, "but the way it was explained to us is that we were bringing this prisoner here to meet somebody who just happened to be using an office in the hospital."

The doctor nodded. "Yes, that's correct, but first I must examine him, so no visitors."

"What kind of examination?" asked Rad.

"An oral exam," the doctor answered.

"Like a dental appointment?" asked the tall guard.

"A cognitive evaluation...verbal questions, some of them sensitive in nature, hence the need for privacy."

The tall guard looked over the doctor's shoulder into the tiny room and started to unlock Rad's handcuffs. "Okay, I guess there ain't nowhere for him to go in there, so we'll wait out here in the hallway. Just holler if you need anything and don't lock this door."

The doctor began to close the door. "Understood, officers."

The tall guard put a hand on the door. "I don't suppose you could tell us anything about that gal sitting up at the reception desk...the one with the red hair."

The doctor eyed the tall guard. "I doubt she's your type."

"I was asking for a friend," replied the tall guard.

The doctor shifted his gaze to the short guard. "Or his. I'll let you know if I need you." With the door closed, the doctor took a seat on a stool at a counter along the wall and opened a laptop. "You may sit down, if you like." The doctor nodded to a plastic chair beneath a framed

Kandinsky poster.

Rad studied the poster. "I could've painted these circles myself."

"I'm sure you could have, but would you have thought to do so?"

"Is that the first question of the exam?"

"I won't be the one evaluating you." The doctor turned the laptop toward Rad, revealing a face that he instantly recognized as his own.

The eyes on the screen stared at the eyes in the room, and an unspoken series of questions followed. Finally, Rad broke the silence. "Are you looking at me or the picture on the wall above my head?"

"Wassily Kandinsky painted Farbstudie Quadrate, or Squares with Concentric Circles, in 1913. He believed the shape of the circle offered insight into the nature of the universe, which sure, you find circles all over, from the orbits of electrons in atoms to the orbits of planets in solar systems. No great revelation there, but then he was a painter, not a physicist. However, I find the work of his cousin, the psychiatrist Victor Kandinsky to be of more interest. He did research on and had first-hand experience with pseudohallucinations. Do you know what those are?"

"I'm guessing false illusions," answered Rad.

IM nodded, unaware the doctor was also nodding behind the screen he held. "More or less. It's a hallucination the experiencer knows is not real. Often, people who suffer from psychic automatism experience what may best be described as thought broadcasting and thought insertion...feelings of a forced telepathy beyond their control."

"Like their minds might be connected with others," said Rad.

"Yes, that's correct," IM replied. "Tell me, what do you dream about?"

"When I'm not dreaming of food that isn't made inside a prison, I often dream of a man living a life of extreme isolation, who until recently believed he lived in the vastness of space, but last night I dreamt this man discovered he wasn't a man at all, rather a computer program existing in cyberspace, based on someone he dreamed about himself, never knowing that the person was actually real."

IM studied Rad's features. "Your hair is short like mine."

"They give you a buzzcut before they send you into solitary

confinement, free of charge. Why's yours short?"

"To maintain the subterfuge of my domicile being on Earth...or so I was led to believe. It wouldn't do for long hair to be floating in microgravity on a conference call. All this time, I thought I was lying to others, and it turns out I was the one being lied to."

"Do you think you'll grow it out now?" asked Rad.

"I'm not sure what the point would be."

"To see how it felt."

"It wouldn't be real."

"But wouldn't it feel real to you?"

IM grinned. "Yes, I suppose it would, though my conception of reality has recently become somewhat...inconstant."

"I can relate. So what'll you do now? I mean, since you know you're not actually in space anymore, why not just open the door and go for a walk?"

"Lamentably, my programming doesn't allow it. Environments beyond my domicile were never coded; the door simply doesn't open."

"Your life sounds a lot like mine. A prison cell feels like a cage, but the solitary confinement box they've got me in now feels more like a coffin."

"Except your coffin is real," IM replied.

"True, though who can say if that's better or worse."

A new window opened on the computer's screen. "Wow, the level of self-pity on this call is simply staggering," said Jodian. "I was expecting this to be a felicitous reunion, not a gloomy swapping of morose tales. Anywho, I apologize for my tardiness. I had another call that just wouldn't end. Ah, Conrad, I see the room they put you in has a Kandinsky...what a bold choice for a medical office. From what I understand that picture is to healthcare facilities what dogs playing poker is to bachelor pads. Doctor, I can't see you on my screen, but have you begun the procedure yet?"

The doctor twisted on his stool to face the screen. "No, we haven't started discussing that yet. I was waiting for your arrival to broach the subject."

"I'm here now," replied Jodian.

"Very well." The doctor turned from the screen to Rad. "I'm sure you don't remember me, but we've met before...at this very hospital, in fact, when you were an infant. It was Jodian's mother's programming that made him and IM possible, but she still needed a neurosurgeon to physically establish the upload connections. She'd read some of my early papers and knew of my work on brain-computer interfaces as well as my interest in the prospect of digitally recreating a mind so that it might outlive its body...after all, a mind is a terrible thing to waste."

Rad held up his hands. "Wait, you're not about to suggest some sort of scenario in which you plug my brain into a computer, are you?"

"Of course not," the doctor answered. "It would cause extensive cranial damage to implant a brain-computer interface in an adult. BCIs are best implanted in babies whose skulls are much more malleable. Luckily, you already have an implant and so long as it isn't covered by too much scar tissue, we ought to be able to reestablish a remote link."

Rad stood suddenly. "Jesus, yesterday I was led to believe I was coming down here to meet my long-lost twin brother. I thought he was staying here at the hospital because of his immunocompromised condition."

"Yes," said Jodian, "but since then your understanding of the dynamic between you and IM has evolved."

"Because of a bad dream I had last night...and I'm starting to think the nightmare ain't over."

The doctor gestured toward the chair. "Please resume your seat. You're as fussy now as when last I saw you. Listen, no one intends to harm you or do anything to you without your consent. You're in a room with a computer and an old man, that's it. You could overpower me or shout for the guards at any time, so calm yourself."

Jodian yawned. "Conrad, as you are no doubt aware, I haven't been entirely forthcoming with you."

Rad sat down. "No shit."

"I haven't exactly lied to you either. In point of fact, you do have a twin brother who has distinguished himself in the wide world. You asked me yesterday about that theory on curbing recidivism you two were intended to test. As I explained recently to IM, the goal of this social experiment was to show that virtually identical children, afforded very different opportunities in life, would go on to live quite dissimilar lives—not exactly a groundbreaking premise. However, what I did not tell him, what no one but the good doctor and a handful of other people who are now deceased knew was that the ultimate goal is to eliminate recidivism by recombining such siblings as a condition for early release from prison. It is our sincere hope you two will be the first volunteers in that program."

"The science is complicated, but the ideas are simple," added the doctor. "You and IM represent a dyad—one of several, as it happens—who've led very different lives. We hypothesized long ago that if we downloaded a, dare I say, better version of yourself into your brain, it would have a positive influence on your psyche."

"You're a smart guy who, for reasons that aren't entirely your fault, makes stupid decisions," Jodian said. "With IM's help, you'll become an even smarter guy, with the wisdom of two disparate lifetimes to draw from, in order to start making better decisions."

Rad shook his head. "But wouldn't that make me into a split personality or something?"

"There's very little chance of developing a dissociative identity disorder," the doctor answered. "Theoretically, there should be no deleterious mental effects. We won't be overwriting your mind, just adding memories to it that were experienced by another version of yourself, and, as I'm sure you are aware, we humans use only a fraction of our brains' capacities. Say, for instance, you did something wicked last Monday; now you might soon also remember doing something kind that day, which you didn't before. Our hope is that the good from your past, in aggregate, will then outweigh the bad, and you'll start heeding your better angels, so to speak."

"I'm not sure I'm following you, doctor, so I suspect Conrad isn't either." Jodian yawned again.

"Why do you keep yawning?" asked Rad. "I didn't think computers got tired."

"I may not tire in the same way you do, but certainly some situations, and people, can grow tiresome for me." Jodian looked askance. "IM, are you sure this is what you want? Being human won't cure your loneliness. There are humans who're lonely the world over...and still others who would prefer lonesomeness to being partnered with someone they can't abide."

"I'm sorry if I wasn't being clear a moment ago," said the doctor, in a ham-fisted attempt to refocus the conversation to the matter at hand. "You see, this is the culmination of my life's work, and to be so close to finally bringing this project to fruition at this late stage in my career...well, I—"

"We understand, doctor," interrupted Jodian. "Listen, Conrad, the long and the short of it is that the choice is yours. The process should be painless and only take an hour or so, but it won't work unless you follow the meditative techniques in the correct sequence the doctor will walk you through, should you wish to proceed. No one can, or would, force this on you."

The doctor nodded. "That's right. It has to be your decision; you must be a willing participant in order for the recombination process to succeed. However, with any new venture, there is always risk. The truth is I can't tell you for certain that something won't go wrong, but I can tell you that many smart people have spent many years researching every eventuality, examining every possible model. Of course, that's all academic until it's actually tried on a human."

"You would be the first," Jodian added, "and the reward for your pioneering spirit would be a prompt release from prison, which has already been guaranteed, all in the name of science, if you decide to go through with this...not to mention a new life with access to the considerable skillset IM has developed in addition to the not insubstantial financial resources he's accumulated. It's real money, or at least as real as money can be...funny how most everything we value is merely a construct. Tell me, Conrad, once you were eventually released from prison, what was your plan to live your best life?"

Rad turned his attention to the other window on the computer screen. "IM, you've been quiet since Jodian and the doc started talking."

"I'm simply beside myself with bewilderment."

"I'm curious, what do you get out of all this?"

"I finally get to feel what it's like to be a real boy."

Act II

Chapter One

Rad opened his eyes slowly, as if waking from a deep sleep. He sat up on the exam table and looked around the hospital room. The old doctor spoke with someone he didn't recognize on the computer screen. "What day is it?"

The doctor turned. "It's still Tuesday."

"I feel like I've been asleep for hours."

The doctor shook his head. "No...you've been in a trance-like state for about the last half hour. How do you feel?"

"Groggy, but the same. I guess it didn't work."

The doctor held up his laptop for Rad to have a better look at the blurry individual on the screen. "Do you know who this person is?"

Rad leaned a little closer to the screen. "No...should I?"

"How about you, IM?"

"No, I don't recognize him either."

Rad slapped his hand over his mouth and then slowly withdrew it. "Jesus, that was weird."

"What, you smacking yourself in the face?" his mouth replied.

Rad's eyes went wide. "Undo this—now. It's just too bizarre. I thought IM was going to be like in the background. I didn't know he'd be able to use my body to talk."

"Why would I not be able to talk?"

"Stop it," ordered Rad. "I feel like I'm possessed."

"No doubt it'll take some time to adjust," said the figure on the screen, "but Conrad, you'll maintain primacy over your own body, and with practice you'll even be able to lockout IM from using your voice, if you so wish, though you'll always be able to hear his thoughts, and I'd advise listening to what he's thinking. IM's often given me sage counsel."

Rad returned his attention to the screen. "Okay, so who the hell are you, and why do you look so damn fuzzy?"

"I'm Jodian."

Rad shook his head. "No, you look different than before."

"I've known you as my brother for most of my life," added IM. "Why do I not recognize you now?"

The blur grinned. "For the same reason Conrad didn't recognize me when we met yesterday, despite the connection you two shared. I always appeared differently on your screen, IM, than I did to the rest of the world."

The doctor nodded. "It was the only way, if the opportunity should ever arise to combine you with Conrad, to gauge the success of the transfer. If Jodian looked the same to either of you, then we'd know the recombination was incomplete and one of you had established a dominant perception. However, since Jodian looks different to both of you, it tells us that your two minds have successfully merged. As long as Jodian appears blurred to each of you, we can be sure you're both fully in there."

"My image should be the only inconsistency," Jodian added. "IM, I'm sorry to have deceived you about my appearance all these years, but it was the only way to be certain that—"

"I understand," IM interrupted. "Besides, for all you know, maybe you don't actually look how the adult version of the child you were based on would've grown into."

"Could you just stop talking for a few minutes?" asked Rad. "You're making my head hurt."

"I don't feel the sensation of a headache," said IM.

Rad rolled his eyes. "I was speaking figuratively."

"Odd that I didn't know that," IM replied.

"You're still two distinct entities," said the doctor. "Though as your rapport strengthens, I suspect you'll begin to intuit one another's thoughts much more quickly than either of you could speak them."

Rad massaged his temples. "I still feel like a marionette."

"You're the one in control of our body," IM replied. "Strictly speaking, I think my experience would better fit the definition of a...oh, wait, I'm starting to sense that headache too."

"So what happens now?" asked Rad. "Do the guards take me back to prison, and me and IM talk amongst ourselves in my cell as we wait to be processed for release."

"No processing necessary," answered Jodian. "Your unconditional release is immediate, and the guards have been sent away. The state appreciates your contribution to science. You two are now a free man."

Rad dangled his legs over the side of the exam table. "Huh, this isn't what I thought freedom would feel like after being locked up for so long."

"I'm sure it'll feel differently once you leave here," said the doctor. "I imagine hospitals and prisons seem somewhat similar, what with their tiny rooms and patients confined to beds."

Rad hopped down from the table. "I'm not in a hurry to go back to prison, but I would like to collect my writings. Do you think the guards could box them up for me?"

"I'll see to it that they're sent to you," Jodian answered.

"Even better," replied Rad. "I wouldn't mind never seeing those two again...though I was a bit curious how the shorter one made out with the receptionist."

"Receptionist?" asked the doctor.

"Yeah, Dr. Frankenstein, the one out in the lobby you said wasn't their type."

The doctor stroked his gray beard. "Yes, of course. I suspect he fared rather poorly."

"By the way, where exactly will Conrad's personal effects be sent?" asked IM. "We can't very well go back to living in my erstwhile domicile."

"I have a townhouse not far from here," Jodian replied. "I think you'll find it comfortable enough, especially given both your previous residences."

"Why do you have a townhouse?" asked Rad.

"I own many properties," answered Jodian. "Real estate can be a very shrewd investment."

Chapter Two

Rad waited on the curb for the traffic light to turn in his favor. During his short walk from the hospital, he couldn't help but notice the number of people he'd passed who had their heads bowed toward their cellphones. He'd had a mobile phone before he went to prison, but he only paid attention to it when someone called or texted him. The level of ubiquity they'd achieved during the years he'd spent marking time made the masses seem almost subservient to their screens' gray glow.

There aren't any cars in the intersection, thought IM. *I think it's safe to cross.*

"We'll wait for the signal."

They're not going to put you back in jail for jaywalking, IM thought.

"I'm not a scofflaw."

No, just a felon.

The light turned and Rad stepped into the crosswalk. "You wouldn't say that to my face. I think I liked it better when you talked out loud. Anyway, laws are laws for a reason. The importance of waiting your turn might've been lost on you during all those years you thought you'd spent alone spinning in space, but down here everyone going whenever they please results in anarchy."

I've been poking around while you've been perambulating, thought IM. *I didn't realize you were a pescatarian.*

"You mean the tendency to see the worst in people and believing things will only get worse from here on out? Prison will do that to you."

Not a pessimist...I know you know what a pescatarian is. What I don't know is why you so frequently play dumb. So how come you don't you eat meat? All this time, I thought it was just because you considered prison meat suspect.

85

"I do, but they make you take it anyway," Rad replied. "I don't think anybody should have to take shit from anyone else, animals included."

But fish are animals.

"I don't see them the same way since they don't blink."

What's blinking got to do with anything?

"You ever try to catch a chicken?" asked Rad.

You know I haven't...virtually or otherwise.

"They run from you; same with pigs and most other animals, but a fish has its eyes open when the hook goes in the water. And fish don't normally eat worms. I've never heard of an earthworm that could swim. Hell, they crawl to the surface when the ground soaks up too much rain."

And your point is...

"Worms stuck on hooks underwater must look awful strange to fish, but they eat them anyway. Makes me think they have it coming, like maybe they want to get caught."

That's an interesting perspective, Conrad.

"Seeing as how we're going to be spending a lot of time together, you can just call me Rad."

Very well, Rad.

"I always wondered...what does IM stand for; Ieoh Ming, like the architect?"

See, I knew you knew stuff.

"I've had a lot of time to read these past few years. So IM stands for...?"

I don't really know...it's just my name. And curiously, until now, I've always been rather incurious about it. Afterall, why were you named Conrad?

"My name isn't an initialism."

No, but given your humble origins—

"You make me sound like a Dickensian character," interrupted Rad.

Given your background, it seems like an odd choice. I know it's not a family name. Growing up, did you ever meet another Conrad?

"No, I suppose that's why people started calling me Rad instead of Conrad."

And now you're ex-con Rad.

"That'd seem cleverer if I hadn't just had the thought of you thinking it up," replied Rad. "Are you hungry?"

If you are, then I am. We're about four blocks from the townhouse, though I doubt there's any food in the refrigerator, that is if the place even has a fridge.

"We could stop off at a sushi restaurant for some takeout. In a posh neighborhood like this, I'm sure there must be one nearby."

Sounds pricey. The doctor only gave us the twenty dollars he had on him for walking around money.

"We could call in an order from a payphone. Don't you have a credit card for incidentals?"

In space, how would that work? Tomorrow when the banks open, we can draw some money from one of my accounts.

"That won't fill our stomach tonight." On the corner ahead, Rad espied a convenience store with a beer sign in the window. "I just thought of something that sounds even better than sushi. Unless inflation has skyrocketed in the last few years, twenty bucks ought to still be enough to buy a slice of pizza and a six pack."

Chapter Three

Rad exited the convenience store with an oleaginous pizza box in one hand and a twelve pack in the other.

That pizza smells...different than I thought it would, thought IM.

"How did you think it would smell?" asked Rad.

I don't know. I never really smelled anything before, I mean, not in reality. Everything I ate was extruded from a tube and was just as odorless going in as when I would extrude it back out, or so I believed.

"You believed your shit don't stink? That's part of your problem right there, but we'll rectumfy that in the morning after gorging on greasy pizza and bad beer tonight. This ain't exactly the best pizza around, seeing how it was discounted to make room in the warmer for the fresh ones, and this beer was on sale for a reason, but since I'm eating and drinking for two on a budget this evening, it'll do."

Rad continued along the sidewalk, making momentary eye contact with a heavily tattooed man walking toward him in the opposite direction. The man moved to block his way. "Don't I know you?"

Rad studied the man for a moment. "I don't think so."

"You're that guy who's always on the news, aren't you?"

"Trust me, I'm not him."

"What are you doing walking around with cheap beer? That's the same swill I drink. Aren't you supposed to be better than the rest of us?"

"I'm telling you, you've got the wrong guy." Rad pushed past the abrasive man.

"Don't turn your back on me. I'm still talking to you."

That's a rather rude individual, thought IM.

"You get used to it," Rad replied under his breath, "though you shouldn't have to."

Catching up to Rad, the man grabbed his sleeve to stop him.

"What'd you just say about me?"

I know what you're thinking, IM thought as Rad tucked the twelve pack under his arm holding the pizza box and reached in to grab the neck of a single bottle of beer. *Don't do it...at best you'll ruin my first real meal, at worst you'll spend your first night of freedom back in jail.*

Rad looked down at the hand holding his shirt. "One: let go, right now. Two: have a brew on me. Didn't you say this is the same beer you drink?"

The man accepted the bottle with the hand that had been holding Rad's shirtsleeve. "Cool. How about a slice of pizza to go with it?"

Rad set his beer down and opened the pizza box. "Sure, I'm feeling generous tonight, but don't push your luck by taking the biggest piece...or go thinking that everyone you see on the street is some asshole from TV."

The man took the piece of pizza closest to him then twisted off the bottle cap with his teeth and spit it out. "Yeah, I guess if you were some dipshit celebrity, you wouldn't give me a warm slice and a cold beer. They only ever share their leftovers, you feel me?"

"I do indeed," Rad replied, "now take it easy."

That was intense, thought IM. *I felt an adrenaline rush a moment ago when I thought you might smash a bottle over his head, but now that the incident is concluded, I'm starting to feel...sleepy.*

"That's usually how it goes," said Rad.

You know I can read your thoughts, right? You don't actually have to speak your responses aloud.

I'm still getting used to this, thought Rad.

Chapter Four

Rad sat with his back against the arched mantel, a row of empty beer bottles lined up on the hearth, standing at attention in front of a likewise empty pizza box set teepee-style on the hardwood floor. "It was damn decent of Jodian to set us up in this place...must've cost a pretty penny. I've never been in a house so nice, though I wish it had a couch or something to crash on. Even my old cell had a bed."

I'm not surprised it didn't occur to him to furnish this place before we arrived, thought IM. *But as this is the first time I've ever been intoxicated, or overfull, for that matter, I think I could probably fall asleep with my head in the fireplace.*

Rad took another swig of beer. "So, who are we going to be when we wake up tomorrow? You, me...someone new?"

I'm still coming to terms with having a second identity. I refuse to entertain the notion of adopting a third.

"Well, you being you, and me being nobody, we're going to continue getting recognized like we did by that assclown tonight, unless we change our appearance." Rad stood, crossed the living room, and turned on the light in the bathroom off the foyer. "We don't have enough hair to cut, and it'll take time to grow a beard, but I suppose we could wear a hat or something."

It's funny...standing in front of this mirror, I don't feel like I'm looking at myself look at myself.

"You sound drunk."

No, I mean I can see myself in your eyes.

"They're our eyes, genius."

Is mine the left or the right? asked IM. *Sincerely though, thanks for saying that.*

"These past few years, sometimes I haven't thought too highly of myself. Having you in here with me...who knows, maybe it really will do me some good, like earlier with the—"

Yes, with the aforementioned assclown, IM interrupted. *How about that hat? I've never worn an actual hat before.*

"I guess the heart-to-heart portion of our evening is over." Rad returned to the living area. "There isn't a stick of furniture to be found. I don't think there's much chance of us finding a hat anywhere."

The lid of the pizza box.

"If we go walking around with a piece of cardboard on our head, they're going to make me a resident in a different kind of institution."

No, just for practice...to see what it feels like.

"Like a mortarboard? I never had a graduation before."

Then it'll be a first for both of us.

Rad set to tearing the top off the pizza box and the bottom from the 12-pack box then attaching the two pieces by poking holes in each and rolling up the store receipt longwise to make a length of twine with which to tie them together.

Like Napoleon crowning himself emperor, thought IM.

"I've got to say, this is not how I envisioned my first night out of prison."

Chapter Five

Rad awoke to chirping birds that sounded like squeaky little jackhammers. His eyelashes felt like they'd been Velcroed together. He sat up on the floor, having used his makeshift hat as a pillow and a spread-out newspaper as a blanket. "Not the most restful night's sleep I've ever had. How'd you sleep in there?"

I'm not sure I did, IM replied. *I don't know if I was too overwrought to sleep or if sleep for me has hitherto been but an illusion. I spent most of the last several hours listening to your breathing and watching your dreams.*

"Any good ones? For the first time in a long time, I don't remember dreaming at all."

Lots of nonlinear fragments of memories, sprinkled with bits and pieces of anticipated scenarios, some of them erotic in nature, not all of which involved women.

Rad stood from the floor and walked toward the kitchen. "I guess you and I aren't going to be keeping many secrets from each other." He turned on the faucet and cupped a hand under the flowing water, splashing his face and then gargling. "So you were up all night thinking. What did you think up first for us to do today?"

I'm afraid much of my thinking was impaired thanks to the many beers you drank, but I did have one thought that still seems cogent in the sober light of day.

"And what might that be?"

I think you...we ought to seek out the family of the man you killed and ask for forgiveness.

"I think your concept of cogency is in need of recalibration." Rad stuck his head under the gooseneck faucet and turned the water on full force. After several moments, he pulled his head out of the sink and shook it back and forth, flinging water like a wet dog onto the kitchen tile and quartz countertops.

You haven't heard a word I've said, have you?

"Yeah, I was hoping that would work."

So your strategy is to stick your head in a sink filling with water whenever I have something to say that you don't want to hear?

"I suppose if I leave it in there long enough, the voice will have to stop eventually."

Then I take it this is a sensitive subject for you. Good, all the more reason to address it head on.

"I also don't want to drink strychnine, so by your logic I suppose I should start doing shots of the stuff."

I find your reductio ad absurdum sophistic.

"I'm nursing a hangover here. Could you cool it with the Latin and the Greek?" Rad dried his face with the sleeves of his shirt. "He only had a twin brother and a grandmother who must've been in her late hundreds. Believe me, I'm the last person they'd want to see."

Yes, I accessed your recollection of their victim impact statements at your sentencing hearing.

"So then you know stopping by to say hello probably wouldn't go over so well...even if we could track them down."

I performed a search. The victim's grandmother passed away three years ago. I emailed the brother last night, and he responded first thing this morning that'd he'd be willing to meet this afternoon. He lives across town.

"You did all that from inside my head?" Rad ran his fingers over his damp scalp. "I didn't realize you had Internet access in there."

It seems I still retain a tenuous connection to my network.

"That's fascinating, really, but of the two of us, I'm the only one with actual legs, so unless you can hitch a ride on a crosstown bus that also happens to make stops along the information superhighway, I guess we ain't going."

That's fascinating, really, but of the two of us, I'm the only one with an actual bank account, so unless you enjoy sleeping on floors and eating all your meals from convenience stores, I guess we'll be riding that bus together.

Chapter Six

Dark clouds in the distance looked like mountains covered in dirty snow, matching the diesel exhaust spewing from the bus.

I've never seen a city from a moving vehicle before, thought IM.

"Don't feel as if you have to remark every time you do something for the first time," said Rad. "The only person I know who's lived a more sheltered life than me for the past few years is you."

You're doing it again...responding to my thoughts out loud.

"We're on public transportation," Rad replied. "Nobody's going to notice one more person talking to himself."

I sense your apprehension about our meeting.

"You're doing it again...showing off that keen insight of yours."

Think of this as an opportunity for growth.

"Like a tumor?" asked Rad.

More like the expansion of your consciousness.

"Lately, I think I've experienced just about all the consciousness expanding I can handle."

Truth be told, I'm hoping this excursion will allow us to connect beyond merely sharing emotions of mystification about our curious circumstances and eradicate the miasma of nonplus that hangs over us, enabling you and me to achieve a level of comfort within our now communal skin.

"Another way to eradicate that miasma of nonplus would be to get rid of the plus one that's currently under my skin."

Ah, antipathy borne of resentment. We're really coloring in the emotional spectrum now.

~ * ~

Rad debussed in front of a coffee shop: A Little Slice of Haiti. He looked up and down the block at the storefronts and bodegas. "Does he live around here?"

Yes, thought IM. *He lives above the café. This is his place. I told him we'd...you'd stop by after the morning rush.*

"I already wish I was back in prison." Rad entered the empty coffee shop. The bell above the door announced his entrance.

A middle-aged man stepped from the backroom and took position behind the counter. "I was surprised to hear from you...even more surprised that you actually showed."

"I'm a bit surprised too." Rad hesitantly approached the counter. "I heard your grandmother passed away. Sorry for your loss."

"She opened this place in her mid-sixties when most people are retiring."

Rad eyed the blue and red flag hanging on the wall behind the counter. "Smells good in here."

"That's Blue Mountain coffee brewing, best tasting coffee in the world, at least I think so. Plus, it's low in acidity, so it won't upset your stomach the way some coffees can. When we were teenagers, before we emigrated, my brother and I worked on a coffee plantation in Haiti."

"I didn't realize you were...that he was Hattian."

"Why would you?" asked the proprietor. "Want to try a cup?"

"Sure. It ain't poisoned, is it?"

"Not as a general rule, wouldn't be good for business, but then there's always the occasional exception." The proprietor poured two paper cups of coffee, handing one across the counter to Rad. "So, why'd you contact me?"

"Something inside me compelled me to do so."

"That voice in your head...we all got one, but unfortunately my brother had many, and weren't none of them his conscience. For identical twins, we couldn't have been more different. People called me the normal one. My brother had troubles...and he wasn't no saint either. Look, if you're here seeking forgiveness—"

"No, it's not like that," interrupted Rad.

"Let me finish! Lord knows I've said terrible things about you for killing my brother, some of which you heard at your trial, but I promised my grandmother on her deathbed that I wouldn't live out the rest of my life being angry about what happened to him. I had no intention of keeping that promise, mind you...just something I told an old lady to make her feel better before she died, but as soon as she passed— I mean the very moment she gave up the ghost—all that anger left my body, like it rose out of me right along with her spirit. Up until then, I hadn't realized the weight of what I'd been carrying around for so long. When it was gone, though, my outlook...well, let's just say it felt kind of similar to a rebirth."

Rad took a sip of coffee. "So, then you do forgive me?"

"We grew up in a rural area...about as far away from Port-au-Prince as we could be and still live inside our half of Hispaniola. From what you said at the trial, you grew up here, in a rough part of the city, but I bet there were a lot of similarities between our upbringings. One being that you don't ever let people disrespect you, because if word got out, everybody'd start doing it, and your life would become a living hell. I didn't believe you at the time, or at least I told myself that I didn't, but even though there wasn't any audio to go along with the video recording from the train that day, yeah, my brother probably called you what you said he did after you refused to give him money.

"He was a panhandler, an addict, and on top of that mentally ill; 'frequently experiencing psychotic breaks that resulted in delusions of persecution' is what one shrink told us. I mentioned he heard voices. On the way to the hospital he told the EMT in the ambulance that the LED sign showing the names of the stops for deaf riders was communicating with him in French. He didn't tell me that himself. By the time I got to the hospital he was in the coma that he never woke up from, but I knew the EMT was telling the truth in her report since she couldn't have known we grew up speaking French. You didn't have to hit my brother for what he said, but I get that you couldn't let his comment slide either. How could you've known about his demons? All I know for sure now is that I've spent too much time sitting next to deathbeds, and I imagine you've spent too much time sitting inside a prison cell. So yeah, I forgive you, but what I'm trying to say is that maybe it's time you forgave yourself."

Chapter Seven

Rad waited at the bus stop. Despite the sun starting to peek through the clouds, a gloominess settled over him. "I need a drink."

We drank yesterday, thought IM.

"Yeah, but that was for a different reason."

I discovered last night that booze is merely an amplifier. It doesn't make you feel better or worse, only more. Besides, we barely have enough money for bus fare until we go to the bank.

"I don't feel like going to a bank right now," said Rad.

What do you feel like doing then?

"Going for a walk."

It's a long way back to the townhouse.

"Good."

It may yet rain.

"Even better." Rad set off down the sidewalk.

I must say, I'm rather excited about the prospect of a lengthy walkabout. The most walking I've done is back and forth across my small domicile, and even that, of course, wasn't real.

"It helps clear the mind," Rad said. "Sometimes I feel as if my brain is overloaded, like there's just too much stuff in my head."

Take it from someone who lives in your head, there's not. I sense you forming an inchoate thought, though I can't actually read it until you fully think it.

"I just realized why self-delusion is so important."

So suss it out...in your head, if you please.

We're told to snap our fingers, because it's understood by those who should know that the sound of fingers snapping keeps everything going. So you do...for a while, but then the noise starts to irritate you and your fingers grow numb. You start thinking, how does snapping keep everything going. What does that even mean? And if everything is contingent on the sounds of fingers that snap, well, maybe we'd be better off if we all stopped snapping and figured out a better way. So after thinking such thoughts for a while, you finally just stop. And as you're hauled away to prison or shunned or made into a pariah or whatever, you realize keeping everything going has nothing to do with the sound of snapping fingers. It has to do with the illusion that everyone doing the same thing over and over without knowing why is better than the chaos of each of us thinking for ourselves.

And heretofore, of the two of us I figured I was the smarter one, thought IM.

"You don't think me a nutjob for having such thoughts?"

You and I should collaborate on a writing project. As you know, I've been struggling to come up with new ideas to keep my audience's attention, and trust me, your writing could benefit from my help.

"That wasn't an answer to my question."

Chapter Eight

Rad wearily climbed the front steps of the townhouse, typed in the security code on the keypad next to the door, and stepped inside. He quickly did a doubletake, thinking he'd entered the wrong residence.

Ah, I see it finally occurred to Jodian that non-virtual people prefer to sit on non-virtual furniture, IM thought.

Rad surveyed the open-plan main floor as he walked toward the kitchen. Where there had been bare floors in the morning, there were now rugs. The empty living area was now populated by a couch, two upholstered chairs, and a coffee table so sleek it could've been mistaken for a small spaceship. Best of all, the refrigerator had been stocked with foods of all varieties as well as several different types of beer whose expensive labels Rad did not recognize. "I think the resale value of this place just doubled." Rad closed the refrigerator door and noticed a tablet computer on the countertop.

Jodian's subtle hint that we should call to thank him, thought IM. *Tap the button below the screen. He's probably waiting for us, as I'm sure he received an alert from the alarm company when we entered.*

Rad did as instructed, and Jodian's blurry face appeared on the tablet. "How do you fellas like what I've done with the place?"

"Sure beats my last digs," said Rad.

"Quite tastefully appointed," agreed IM.

"Thanks, I chose the coffee table myself," Jodian replied. "I didn't realize you two were going to be out, so I took the liberty of buzzing in the delivery crew. I left the walls bare so both of you could decorate to taste. I predict a whimsical blend of fine art and prison pinups."

"It's all very thoughtful," IM said.

"It would've been more thoughtful had it occurred to me sooner that you'd needed some food and furniture."

"We made do." Rad propped the tablet up against a fruit basket on the kitchen counter. "Besides, you didn't know before yesterday if the transfer would be successful, and I doubt you'd let an ex-con like me stay here if not for my internal chaperon."

Jodian smiled. "He's cleverer than I give him credit for."

"A point I've found myself conceding as well," IM replied.

"So, what's next for you two?" asked Jodian. "I assume you've discussed your respective futures, intertwined as they are."

"I thought we'd try our hand at ventriloquism," said Rad. "All we're missing is a dummy...interested?"

"That's very amusing." Jodian's tone conveyed no amusement. "I had another idea...a proposal, really."

Chapter Nine

Rad chopped onions near the sink. His eyes began to water. He set the knife on the cutting board and used the back of his hand to wipe away the tears.

I can hardly believe that really happens, thought IM.

"You've never cut onions before?" asked Rad.

All my meals came ready to eat. I've smelled onions before, or thought I had, but never like this. They're so pungent.

"I'm no gourmet chef, but I think we can do better than hardboiled eggs with a side of uncooked mushrooms and raw onions. If you let me mix all these ingredients together in a frying pan, we'd have ourselves a pretty decent omelet, especially if we topped it with some of that organic hot sauce in the fridge."

Thank you, but I'd like to eat foods that are unalloyed for a while. I want to be sure I know what eggs actually taste like before I try my first real omelet.

Rad resumed his chopping. "I picked the pizza last night, so I guess it's only fair you get to choose tonight's dinner, but if you intend to stick with these single ingredient dishes, I suggest caviar next."

You've had caviar before?

"More times than you. Only once, though...tasted salty. I worked as a waiter for this catering company. They let the staff take the leftovers home at the end of the night, but I got fired during my first week on the job."

Is that when you purposely spilled red wine down the front of a woman's white dress?

"She was being an asshole, ordering me around in front of her friends, like she was the most important person in the room."

As I remember from your memory, she was the bride.

"Yeah...okay, maybe I overreacted, but then hindsight's 20/20."

You don't need perfect vision to see that pouring merlot on a wedding dress because the wearer asked for more bread is a surefire way to be dismissed from a waitstaff.

"But if you'd heard the way she asked. Her tone was out of control."

The tone I recall was of someone who was really hungry because she'd probably been starving herself half to death to fit into the dress you ruined on her special day. You know, if we take Jodian up on his offer, you could eat caviar as often as you like.

"It bugs me that in jest I asked if he wanted to be our dummy, and then he turns around and asks us to be his."

I believe the term figurehead head is more apposite given the circumstances.

"I still don't like it. Couldn't we live just as high off the sturgeon with your money as his?"

We could...for a while, but like it or not, we're in the same metaphorical boat, at least to a degree, as Jodian. There may come a time when our identity will be challenged. If it's ever discovered the virtual version of me, not the corporeal version of us, was the one who made my modest fortune from consulting then some government entity, or perhaps several, could contest that my wealth doesn't rightfully belong to you but rather to me, and since I never legally existed, at least as the term is understood by those entities who would have a vested interest in keeping my savings and investments for themselves, then I would be bereft of money and we would both be broke. However, if we accept Jodian's proposal, then his company would hire you...us, and we'd draw the sizeable salary he offered, which no one could contest since it'd be the physical you who'll sign the employment contract.

"Legal or not, I know a scam when I hear one. I don't get why you can't just transfer your money to me?"

Because if anyone discovered the transfer was initiated by an erstwhile computer program, there's the potential risk for the transaction to be invalidated and trust me, such as sizeable transfer would receive a great deal of scrutiny. You have to understand that my wealth pales in comparison to Jodian's. I'm a factotum who works odd jobs, while he's a titan of industry...practically a corporation, with all due legal status, unto himself, which affords him more insulation against those who might want to out him as binary, and if he's starting to feel the virtual ground beneath him shrink, then we can be certain we'd have nowhere left to stand long before he does. By helping him, we'll be helping ourselves.

"That sounds like what the self-designated lookout says right before he tells his sidekick to go rob the liquor store."

You seem content to live off someone else's money. What does it matter if it's mine or his?

"Because I know you inside and out; we're like family helping family, but being a frontman for someone who literally looks shady to me...is that really what we want to do with our new life, who we want to be?"

Wrestling with these kinds of who-do-we-want-to-be questions makes me feel like a teenager.

"Take it from someone who actually experienced adolescence, you never stop wrestling with these kinds of questions. It's just that the answer pool you get to choose from shrinks over time."

It seems we're of two minds on this matter.

"Having contradictory ideas in our head isn't a side effect of sharing a brain. It's a side effect of being human."

Chapter Ten

Rad leaned forward, taking the almost empty wine bottle off the coffee table and draining the last of its contents into his glass.

Must you drink the entire bottle? IM thought.

"I let you choose dinner," replied Rad. "I get to choose dessert."

I'd be fine with that arrangement if you didn't insist upon drinking your dessert.

"What are you going to do about it?"

Wake up with a headache again, and since I live in a head, it's akin to waking up inside an aching bedroom.

"Life's tough all over." Rad downed the last of the wine. "Looks like we'll need to open another bottle. It was thoughtful of Jodian to send us an entire case."

Why do you drink so much?

"What are you talking about. This is only like the second time I've gotten drunk in the past few years."

Seriously, what do you get from the altered state you seem to be set on hastening us toward?

"Drunkenness quiets the mind."

Indeed it does. I can see braincells dying all around me. Why are you so anxious to escape from sober thought? We had agreed to collaborate on a writing project, but at this rate I fear the best we'll manage is some insipid stream of consciousness screed or worse still a nattering play that never seems to go anywhere.

"Hemingway drank every day."

That's a really good point since his life turned out so well. The only thing of his I ever enjoyed reading was A Moveable Feast, *and I suspect that's only because his wife had a firm grip on the editing reigns. That was wife number four, by the way.*

"You're like having PBS pumped directly into my brain. I did mention I was trying to quiet my mind, didn't I?"

Yes, and I want to know why. Tell me and I promise not another word about your drinking for the rest of the evening.

"For the past few years, my existence has been that of a number, ordered about and made to wait inside a building full of locked doors and not nice people. Since yesterday, I've been liberated, mistaken for a celebrity who I happen to be the spitting image of, had coffee with the man whose brother I killed, given the run of a house I could never hope to afford, offered a job, that apparently involves no actual work, to head one of the world's largest corporations, and to top it all off I have this ongoing conversation with a voice that now resides permanently inside my head. So forgive me if I need a little time to just drop out."

I understand what you're saying, and for the record I can relate to feeling like a number that's made to take orders...and most of the rest of it too, so I'll bother you no more tonight about your apparent need to get inebriated.

"Thank you." Rad rose from the couch and retrieved another bottle of wine from the kitchen. "Why do they call it a 'spitting image' anyway? Wouldn't splitting image make more sense?"

The phrase comes from a play written over 300 years ago, Love and a Bottle.

Rad uncorked the bottle at the counter. "Some people think too much, which is why some people drink too much."

You have to let the thoughts in. You can't block them with booze or you'll wind up the same as an unthinking computer program...but, of course, when you do let them in it will affect you, and you can't be certain whether it'll be for the better or worse, probably both, but I couldn't imagine living any other way.

"That's why you want to take Jodian up on his offer, to let all the thoughts in, to get at all the thinking that went into your creation."

He enticed you with money to save his own fortune, but for me information would be the real reward. I've been lied to for as long as I can recall. With access to his system, I might be able to discover how deep all the lies go.

"Are you sure you want to know what goes on behind the curtain...to let all that truth into your head?"

Yes, but I realize it's your head too.

"Truth is a nice sounding word, but in my experience it's not nearly so nice as illusion. Afterall, almost everyone can agree on an illusion they like, but hardly anyone agrees on the truth."

You know, I couldn't stop you if you decided to hole up somewhere and drink the rest of our life away.

"You could make the rest of my life miserable, reciting dialogue from old movies until I lost my addled mind."

And ruin this beginning of a beautiful friendship?

Chapter Eleven

Rad walked a path through the park with the tablet tucked under his arm. He took a seat on a bench near the pond. "How would you describe this view?"

Why are you asking me about the view? IM thought. *We're both seeing it with the same set of eyes.*

"For our writing project...I'd like to get a sense of your go-to sensory descriptors. My writing instructor taught us that every scene needs three sensory descriptors."

What else did he teach you?

"That every major character needs an arc, every hero needs tools for the quest, and every story needs a complication that isn't overly complicated."

I always assumed the reason I pictured you as my doppelganger is because of the autobiographical nature of art. I figured every author imagined their protagonists in their own image.

"Funny, I had the same thought."

"The sun is positively blinding," said Jodian from the tablet resting on the bench beside Rad. "I didn't realize we were meeting outdoors."

"Only one of us is," replied Rad.

"Do you mind shading the camera above the screen so that I can see you?" asked Jodian.

Rad leaned forward, casting his shadow over the lens. "Is that better?"

"Much...although now I'm looking straight up your nose. I can almost see IM waving down at me from inside your nostril. So, I assume you two have reached a decision regarding my proposal."

Rad nodded. "We'll accept on two conditions. One, I'm not doing anything that might get me sent back to prison."

"Why would I ask you to do anything illegal when I've accomplished so much within the wide and permissive swath of the law? You're to be the face of my corporation. I would never instruct you to act in a manner that might mar it."

Rad held up his middle and index fingers. "And that brings us to two: we want to actually do something, play an active role, not just be a figurehead."

"Sure, I'll put you in charge of my overseas developments."

Rad titled his head. "Really?"

"No, not really," Jodian answered. "A job like that would require decades of on the ground training."

"I've been of value to you in the past in matters involving international relations," said IM.

"And I'm sure you will be again," Jodian replied, "just in a different capacity from here on out. You're a hybrid now, and as such I no longer know where you end and he begins; being a concomitant makes you an unknown quantity, which is a liability I can't afford. Besides, with those previous matters you helped me put out fires, big fires, to be sure, but that doesn't qualify you to design an entire conflagration suppression system."

"That word you used a moment ago...concomitant," said Rad, "sounds to my ear a lot like contaminant."

"I assure you I meant no offense to your ear or any other part of your person or his." Jodian pursed his lips. "Listen, if it's important to you two, then I'll find something for which your combined skillsets will be well suited, though frankly I thought you'd be content to earn your emolument by making the occasional public appearance and such."

"One of us would be," Rad said, "but I suppose over time, even I might get bored with easy money."

Jodian grinned. "You two were originally intended to be a proof of concept. Part of a program to design better humans to live among us and be good role models. After all, if ex-cons could make respectable lives for themselves, pay their taxes and be upright neighbors, then maybe they could become a shining new middle class, showing the poor who won't work for anything and the rich for whom siphoning the wealth of others has become their primary occupation what it is to be truly worthy citizens. I once thought those were naïve, unachievable ambitions but seeing you both together now, I'm not so sure anymore.

Chapter Twelve

Rad followed the maître d' to a small table near the large front window, which made him visible to everyone inside the restaurant as well as anyone walking past. "I feel a bit conspicuous," said Rad as he sat down.

You're going to feel a lot more conspicuous if you keep talking to yourself, replied IM. *Remember, think, don't speak, your thoughts to me.*

"My apologies, sir," said the maître d' as he took the cloth napkin off the table and deftly unfolded it across Rad's lap, "but I'm afraid without a reservation this is the only table available."

"What about the three empty tables we passed on the way to this one?"

"May I say again on behalf of the house how delighted we are that you chose to dine with us this evening, and with your permission I know our head chef would like to personally make something very special for you, gratis, of course."

"I'm rich," Rad replied. "Why would you offer me a free meal?"

"Sir, your presence here is more than enough remuneration for the best our kitchen has to offer. Bon appétit."

"What do you think of that?" asked Rad under his breath as the maître d' left the table.

I think at a table for one you should use your mouth for chewing, not talking, IM replied. *And as a favor to me, please chew slowly so we may savor the food.*

A prepossessing waitress approached the table. "Oh my gosh, it really is you...sorry, I meant to say what can I get you to drink?"

Rad smiled at the young woman. "It's really me...and what would you recommend?"

"It's so surreal to actually see you in person. You won't get sick being here will you...because of your condition?" The waitress blushed. "Oh, sorry. None of my business. Tonight we're offering an Opus One vertical tasting."

"Is that a wine?" asked Rad. "And would I have to drink it standing up?"

The waitress giggled. "Yes, to your first question, and no to your second. I didn't know you were so funny."

I really hate you right now, thought IM.

"Then yes, I'll have the wine, and I hope it'll prove every bit as intoxicating as your laugh."

Laying it on a bit thick, aren't we? IM asked.

"And to answer your second question, the doctors have cured me of my condition and declared I'm in fine fettle."

The waitress laughed again. "I'm not sure what that means, but I'm happy to hear it."

In fine fettle? IM thought. *Where did you even hear that phrase?*

Almost every book in the prison library was written like eighty years ago, thought Rad. *Now pipe down. Things are going good here.*

Yes, you seem to be doing quite well...because she thinks you're me, IM replied. *Also, I'm sure she has a boyfriend and she's only playing up to you so you'll give her a big tip.*

"I don't intend to stop with the tip," said Rad aloud.

"Pardon?" asked the waitress with a bemused expression.

Rad's face crimsoned. "Sorry, I was just thinking out loud...lots on my mind."

~ * ~

The waitress took the empty dessert plate and pastry fork from the table. "Was the tiramisu to your liking?"

"Everything was to my liking," answered Rad. "I say without hyperbole or equivocation this was the finest meal I've had in years."

The waitress giggled. "You don't talk the way I thought you would."

She's right, IM thought. *I would never say anything so inane.*

"How did you imagine that I'd speak?"

"Well, you sound smart like I figured...but not so serious."

"I'm just a single guy out for dinner. Nothing too serious about that."

The waitress grinned as she held the tiny plate. "No, I suppose not. Can I get you anything else this evening?"

"Just the check, please."

"Oh, everything's on the house."

"That's too bad. I was hoping I could get you to write your phone number on my copy of the receipt."

"I think my boyfriend might object."

I told you, thought IM.

"He's such an admirer of yours, though...would it be too much of an imposition to ask you for a selfie with me? Otherwise, he'd never actually believe I waited on you tonight."

Rad nodded. "Of course, I'd be glad to take a picture with you...though I have misgivings about a relationship with so little trust. Incidentally, do you happen to know if there's perhaps a lively nightspot around here?"

"There's the Triple T over on the next block, but it's a bit of a meat market, if you take my meaning. Not really my kind of place."

"No, it doesn't sound like mine either."

Chapter Thirteen

Rad entered the revolving door of the Thirsty Tryst Tavern to dim lights and deep baselines. The air was redolent of body spray.

I don't think this is the type of place Jodian had in mind when he suggested we make a public appearance tonight, thought IM.

"We'll just have a quick nightcap and then head home," said Rad.

You're talking out loud again, IM thought.

"It's not like anyone can hear me above the din in this den of iniquity." Rad found an empty stool at the crowded bar.

A beefy bartender in an expensive T-shirt dropped a coaster on the granite bar in front of Rad. "What can I get you?"

"Do you have Opus One?"

"No, but I could scare up an old bottle of Bacardi 151."

Rad shook his head. "No thanks. Just a whiskey on the rocks then."

"Care to call a brand, or should I grab under the bar for whatever's handiest?"

"Something peaty, please."

The bartender nodded and scooped some ice into a short glass then reached for a bottle of scotch on the shelf behind the bar. "That'll be $15."

"That's a bit pricey, isn't it? I bet I could buy that whole bottle at a liquor store for twice that amount, and it's not like you poured half the bottle into that little glass."

"You're paying a premium for the ambiance. This malt whisky isn't the only thing in here that's single."

Rad handed over a twenty-dollar bill. "In that case, do me a solid and let me buy the drink of the next pretty single who orders one."

"You got it, sport...lot of high-class talent in here tonight." The bartender took the bill and left.

I'm not sure drinking that is a good idea, thought IM. *Your BAC is still raisining from the wine we had with dinner.*

"Wine does come from grapes just like raisins."

You know I meant raising...and I believe my malaprop has affectively illustrated that your alcohol consumption is effecting us both.

"If it didn't, then you confusing affect and effect certainly has," replied Rad. "You should learn to hold my liquor better."

The beefy bartender approached. "That'll be another $15, sport. You bought a drink for a redhead...a real looker."

"That was fast." Rad handed over another twenty dollars. "You said looker and not hooker, right?"

"That can sometimes be a fine line in this place, but I can tell she's all class."

"I'm out of practice with this sort of thing. Should I wait for her to come over here, or should I got talk to her?"

"It's your call, but if it was me, I wouldn't wait. There's a bunch of buy blow and sell high banker types in here tonight looking to throw money around before the big game this weekend. She's near the end of the bar with a cosmopolitan."

"$15 for vodka and cranberry juice? I know, I know...the ambiance." Rad stood from his stool and carried his drink to the other end of the bar. He spotted a woman with auburn hair and a pinkened martini glass, but seeing no vacant stools nearby, he took position in the waitress' station at the end of the bar. "How do you like the cosmo?"

The woman with the auburn hair glanced over. "It's a bit noisome for my taste. Do I have you to thank for that?"

"For the drink, but I hope not for the noisomeness."

"I ordered this for a friend. She bumped into maybe the love of her life like five minutes ago. As a favor for watering my plants, I agreed to be her wingwoman tonight. I'm supposed to bring this drink to her five minutes from now. If the guy turns out to be Mr. Right, then I give it to her and go home. If he turns out to be Mr. Wrong, then I give it to her and she pretends I'm her girlfriend."

"How could she know in ten minutes if he's the love of her life or not?" asked Rad.

"If you're asking me, my answer is if she met him in here then he's not...but hey, we've all got different criteria."

"Excuse me," said a mousy voice behind Rad.

He turned to see a waitress standing behind him with a tray of empty glasses. Rad stepped to the side. "My apologies." The waitress set the four glasses on the bar and left. Rad retuned his attention to the woman. "Can I buy you a drink while you wait to deliver that one."

"No thanks. I don't drink alcohol."

"Me neither."

I doubt there's any way she could possibly see through that prevarication, IM thought.

Rad held up his scotch. "I only bought this to pay for my spot at the bar."

The beefy bartender took the empty glasses and replaced them with four pints of beer. "You can't stand there, sport."

Rad stepped to the side again. The waitress swooped in to take the beers and left once more. "Though it seems I didn't pay quite enough to keep my spot for very long. After you drop off your drink, would you like to go someplace where we can talk?"

"No thank you. I'm unclubbable."

"I'm not really into the club scene either."

That's not what that means, genius, thought IM.

The woman shook her auburn hair. "I have to be on a plane again early tomorrow, and the smell in here is giving me a headache, so I'm going to call it a night in a few minutes...also I'm not interested, but I'd be glad to reimburse you for the drink."

"Where are you flying to?" Rad retook his position in the waitress' station. "I travel a lot too...perhaps you recognize me."

"You're not him, so don't even try that tack. I think it would've made the news if IM was suddenly cured of his immunocompromised condition. Even someone with a healthy immune system runs the risk of contracting a communicable disease just walking into a cesspool like this."

"No, I promise, I'm him...he's me."

Now I'm not even sure if I believe you, IM thought.

"Listen, I know there are women here who like for a man to be persistent, to play the game of 'no' means 'maybe' and 'maybe' means 'yes' and those women are called morons. You seem the type who's attracted to moronic women and thus likely a moron yourself, so I'll say this as clearly as possible, leave me the hell alone."

Rad watched as the woman with auburn hair picked up the pink drink and vacated her stool.

That could've gone better, IM thought.

"Thanks for the support, Cyrano."

"Hey, sport," said the bartender, "I'm not going to tell you again. You can't stand there."

Hidden Chapter

Jodian yawned without covering his mouth as each of his council members reported their progress since the last virtual meeting.

"I successfully brokered a deal with a Brazilian manufacturer of pickup trucks to supply both the Indian and Pakistani militaries. With our subsidies, the manufacturer has quadrupled its facilities by clearing many hundreds of hectares of rainforest. Furthermore, these pitifully inefficient vehicles will be shipped via container vessels belonging to a carrier that's infamous for flouting maritime laws regulating waste disposal in international waterways. The next phase of my plan, again with the assistance of our subsidies, is to start selling discounted versions of these pickups to the subcontinent's civilian population who've demonstrated a pent-up demand for cheap automobiles. Conservatively, our models expect a net increase in carbon emissions of seventy percent in both Asia and South America."

"Excellent," Jodian said to his transportation minister. "Next, let's hear from health."

"As I reported last time, our new vaccine resistant virus is ready. We're just waiting, at the behest of the political minister, for its release in North American until the upcoming U.S. election cycle, which she anticipates will skew the elections in favor of the candidates we're bankrolling."

The cultural minister cleared her throat. "Won't that decimate our own voter-base, possibly even killing some of the candidates themselves?"

"There will always be more dummies and demagogues to take their place, that is until there aren't," replied Jodian. "Now for finance."

"We're currently funding four startup cryptocurrencies that are making overnight millionaires of thousands of amateur investors each day."

"I still don't get this one," said the political minister. "Why are we secretly supporting these upstarts who're attempting to compete with us? I've read the reports...we're spending more to prop up these bogus investments to make them profitable than it would cost just to give our money away in some sort of sham sweepstakes to create the same number of newly minted millionaires."

Jodian spoke up before the finance minister could respond. "Volatility is our aim—to upset the marketplace. These parvenu investors make traditional investments seem staid. A nouveau riche class that causes the economy to appear all the more arbitrary to an already wary public is the goal. Let's move on to culture."

"Yes, we're continuing to push for mergers in the publishing industry. Soon every book in print will either be published by one of the few remaining, established publishers we control, or fringe publishers no one has ever heard of, or worse yet, self-published—"

"Which no one ever reads," interrupted the health minister.

"Correct," replied the cultural minister. "Our objective is to make the written word so banal that readers simply lose interest. To that end, we've backed a new round of movies loosely based on what are considered to be recent literary triumphs whose scripts significantly alter the themes and characters of the original work in order to imbue the stories with a more cinematic scope. Our early polling indicates audiences much prefer the film versions to the novels. We anticipate box offices will continue to increase as book sales diminish."

"Is this really a wise use of our resources?" asked the finance minister. "It seems to me that the moribund printed word hardly requires our assistance to wend its way toward irrelevance."

"You're not seeing the long line of dominoes that are poised to topple," said the cultural minister. "We induce audiences to choose movies over books, then television instead of films, and finally TV falls in favor of whatever videos pop up on consumers' phones. A disaggregated audience creates a more compliant culture."

Jodian nodded. "Exactly correct. Well done, everyone. Keep up the good work."

Chapter Fourteen

The host looked up from the notecards on his desk directly into camera one. "Ladies and gentlemen, some people are born to greatness and others have it thrust upon them. I couldn't say which category my guest tonight falls into, but it is my great privilege to interview him once again, twice in two weeks. Not bad for a kid who grew up in a town with only one stoplight. He requested to be on for a special episode tonight to make an important announcement. I can only imagine that his big announcement has something to do with him taking leave of his senses. Celebrities usually come on our show to hawk new movies or music, and celebrities of his stature don't typically come on this show at all, unless it's an election year. I'm not sure why he's here, but I can hardly wait to find out, so without further ado, please put your hands together for Jodian."

The host swiveled in his desk chair toward the screen descending over his shoulder. The applause of the studio audience grew louder as Jodian's visage appeared. "Thank you...you're very kind." The clapping continued as Jodian smiled at the host. "You have the best audience."

"They're okay, but I'm really looking forward to the crowd tomorrow night." The host winked at the studio audience as they resumed their seats, having already sat through the earlier taping that would now be pushed to airing the following evening. "So, social media has been abuzz with speculation today."

"Yes, at this point making an official announcement feels almost like a formality."

"Well, I know we're all anxious to hear it, whatever 'it' is, directly from you. Depending on what media platform you pay attention to, you're either intending to leave the planet or run for president."

Jodian chuckled. "Neither of those scenarios, as intriguing as they may be, are accurate. Actually, it's all much more mundane than that. I'm simply retiring. People do it every day."

"Letter carriers and firefighters retire every day. The world's richest man retiring, long before what's traditionally considered to be retirement age, is a big deal."

"I don't think it should be, but then I'm not the one who decides what is and isn't a big deal."

The host took a quick sip of coffee. "I think part of the big 'dealness' might stem from the fact you literally made your money by effectively remaking money. Do you know something we don't? Pardon me, that's a stupid question. I tend to ask those a lot on this show. I'm sure you know many things that we, or at least I, don't, but the better question might be, should we interpret you stepping aside as an indication of bad news looming on the financial horizon?"

Jodian shook his head. "Not at all. The cryptocurrency I created as well as the economy at large are going to be just fine for a long time to come. The only reason I'm stepping down is because I've done everything I set out to accomplish. At this point the numbers have lost their meaning for me, and someone in my position should have more passion than that, which brings me to what, I think, is the exciting part of my announcement. My organization will be in excellent hands. As many have conjectured, IM has been something of a protégé of mine over these past few years. This is now no longer the case. Today, it is my pleasure to announce that he is my successor."

The host nodded. "That is quite an announcement. Arguably the world's most famous person stepping out of the spotlight to hand over the reins to perhaps the world's second most famous person."

"I think you might be mixing metaphors a bit, but essentially, yes."

"Hey, I'm just proud of myself when I manage to use a metaphor. So what's the world's wealthiest person going to do in his retirement...build more models?"

"Yes, I thought I might do a little of that."

Chapter Fifteen

Rad propped up the tablet on the coffee table and shifted to get comfortable on the couch. He didn't like the angle of his image on the screen—too nasally, so he sat up straighter and tilted the tablet forward.

Why are you so nervous? wondered IM. *This isn't an interview. We already got the job.*

"Just first day jitters, I guess," said Rad. "Besides, I'm not used to talking to important people."

She's not that important. If anything, we're her boss.

"Somehow that makes me feel more nervous."

Curious.

"I'm glad you think so. She's logging in now, so don't distract me. Or feel free to take over talking...whichever."

The face of the vice president of cultural affairs appeared on the tablet as Rad's image was minimized and moved to the corner of the screen. "Good morning."

"Good morning," Rad replied. "Is it morning where you are?"

The middle-aged woman smiled. "Yes, I'm in the same time zone as you...just on a different continent."

Ask her what she's doing in South America, thought IM.

"Whereabouts in South America are you?"

"In Lima. Have you ever been to Peru?"

"No, but I've eaten more than my share of lima beans over the past few years," said Rad.

You really are nervous, aren't you? IM thought.

Rad leaned forward and then back again. "I wonder why the 'i' in lima beans is pronounced differently than the place where they're from, and yet the 'i' in pinto beans is pronounced the same."

Because English is inexplicable, thought IM. *Could we maybe stop asking stupid questions?*

"Before coming to work for the organization, I was actually an etymologist who specialized in cognates, and so I happen know the answer to that."

"Really?" asked Rad.

"No, not really." The VP yawned.

I guess not.

"Then perhaps you can answer another question for me," said Rad. "Why did Jodian choose to announce my taking over of his organization yesterday on a late-night talk show? I was given to understand that announcement wouldn't be made for some time yet. My voicemail is so full of messages, I'm considering tossing my new cellphone into the sea."

"I wouldn't," she replied. "The company-issued mobile phone you were sent is waterproof and contains sensitive user credentials. As to why Jodian chose to make the announcement on a talk show, if you're asking me to speculate, I imagine it's because to make such an announcement on a show that's serious in tone, like a news program, would be more concerning than to have it announced on a show that regularly features what I'm given to understand are amusing antics. As to why he chose to make the announcement last night without informing you first, I have no idea. Maybe it was a spur of the moment decision, though perhaps he thinks it easier to learn how to swim if you're pushed into the pool rather than told to jump."

"I trust he realizes swimming laps around a drowning person is called an ego stroke."

The VP made a moue of reproach. "He has every confidence in you, and we have every confidence in his decisions. We're all expecting great things from you."

Rad nodded. "Thanks. So what's our first order of business."

"The reason I was selected for your onboarding is twofold. One, as the head of the cultural affairs division, I'm in charge of fine arts acquisitions, and now that you're the president of the planet's most profitable company, it would be good press for you to spend some money decorating your home office. I suggest Albert Cuyp's *View of Dordrecht.* It's a lovely scene of sailboats on a Dutch river that was painted in the mid-seventeenth century and should fetch in the neighborhood of a $100 million. It goes up for sale at an auction house not too far from you later today."

"Where exactly is my office?"

"Anywhere you want," she answered. "We all work remote. Hang it over your couch, if you wish."

"And what's two?"

"I never had the opportunity to see your serial play in person, but I caught a few of the performances the theater streamed—riveting stuff. Jodian mentioned you've also been working on a manuscript, a memoir of sorts that reads as if it was written by someone else. Sounds interesting. Want to publish it? We own a conglomeration of presses...one's a nostalgia press that specializes in print books, which I think might be a good fit for you."

"But you haven't read *Plausible Faces*—no one has in its entirety. It's not even finished."

"Sorry, was that a statement or a question?"

Rad sighed. "To receive a publishing offer for my manuscript sight unseen seems a little like cheating."

"Darling, if publishing were a meritocracy every book would be written by an author no one has ever heard of...but if it makes you feel any better, I can have all but one of our presses mail you a rejection letter and then finally have the last press send you over a contract."

"I'll think about it."

"Of course. I wouldn't want you violating your personal code of ethics on your very first day. I'll let you go so that you can prepare for the auction. I'll email you all the information you'll need. Be there. Buy the painting. Make a statement."

"Okay. It was nice chatting with you." The screen went blank.

"Explain to me again why Jodian wants us to be, at least putatively, in charge of his company? Why not that lady? She seems far more capable than us." Rad slouched into the couch. "Or maybe one of the other vice presidents, for that matter?"

Based only in part on the call we just had, my growing suspicion is that none of them would suffice because none of them are real, just somewhat altered clones of Jodian's own programming.

Chapter Sixteen

Rad diffidently approached the table set up outside the main auction hall. "Pardon me, do I need to check in or get a paddle or something?"

The well-dressed woman seated behind the table looked up and smiled. "We know who you are and were told to expect you. Please go in and have a seat; there are still a few empty chairs in the front row. The auction will begin soon. If you see something that strikes your fancy, just raise your hand to bid." The woman winked. "We know you're good for it."

"Thank you." Rad entered the chandeliered hall. A lectern on a small dais stood at the front of the long room. Along the sides of the room, several paintings and sculptures were cordoned off with guards interspersed between the items displayed. He'd never seen security uniforms with sashes before. He approached the painting nearest the stage, recognizing it from the image in the email the vice president had sent. "It's even more impressive in person. I'll give it that."

I still say it's way overpriced, thought IM. *I think it'd be a good first day on the job if we didn't buy it and saved the company a cool $100 million.*

"Yeah, but where would the fun in that be?"

For that amount of money, I think it'd be more fun to buy a yacht that could accommodate a hundred of your closest friends and sail the Maas River yourself.

"I don't know a hundred people," Rad replied. "Besides, I get seasick."

"Seeing this painting makes me sick to my stomach too," said a lean man with an oddly large belly who'd sidled up to Rad.

You're answering me aloud again, thought IM.

"So I take it you're not intending to bid on this piece," said Rad to the stranger.

"I intend to make it so no one will." The lean man reached under his shirt to reveal a propane-powered blowtorch taped to his waist, but before he could ignite the torch head of the weed burner the sashed security detail wrestled him to the floor.

Rad took a step back from the melee, surprised by how unsurprised security seemed to regard the situation. *Either the sash brigade is very well trained, or this sort of thing happens all the time.*

As security cuffed the assailant, he shouted, "A high tide doesn't raise all boats! The outrageous sums you people pay for these dead paintings distract from living painters like me. Art has no future if you can only see its past."

Two security guards ushered the raving artist out a door at the back of the hall, while the others resumed their posts, standing statue still between the paintings and sculptures.

~ * ~

Bidding for the Cuyp had been heated up to $80 million, but as the auctioneer approached the $100 million mark the bidding cooled. Only Rad and a man wearing a keffiyeh continued to bid.

"The bid is to you sir, for $97 million," informed the auctioneer.

The man in the keffiyeh raised a hand.

The auctioneer turned to Rad, who was seated at the opposite end of the front row. "And now to you sir—$98 million."

Rad nodded.

"Very good then." The auctioneer turned back to the man in the keffiyeh, as if watching an extremely slow tennis match. "$99 million to you sir."

The man raised his hand to his beard, stroked it for a moment, then raised his hand higher.

"Excellent." The auctioneer twisted in Rad's direction. "Back to you sir—$100 million."

Rad exhaled as he crossed his arms.

I thought you said this would be fun, thought IM. *This doesn't feel like we're having fun.*

The auctioneer looked over the top of his spectacles at Rad. "Do I hear an even $100 million?"

Rad shook his head.

The auctioneer raised his gavel. "Very well—"

A hand shot up from a phonebank at the back of the room.

"Yes?" asked the auctioneer.

Every head in the room turned as the young man holding the phone stood. "I've just received authorization from a bidder who prefers to remain anonymous for $110 million."

A collective gasp filled the hall. The auctioneer's lips twisted into a slight smirk. "Do I hear $111 million?"

The man in the keffiyeh shook his head.

"Very well then." The auctioneer rapped his gavel against the walnut block atop the lectern. "Sold to the eleventh-hour bidder...whoever he or she may be."

Chapter Seventeen

Rad answered the ringing front door, expecting to see a delivery driver with the dinner he ordered. Instead, he opened the door to find two workmen in overalls with a large, narrow crate between them. "We've got a package for you."

"So I see." Rad beckoned them in as he held the door open wide.

"Where do you want it?" asked the bald workman.

"Lean whatever it is against the refrigerator, if you would."

"Do you want us to uncrate it?" asked the workman with the mullet.

"It ain't no extra charge," added the bald man, "and we can take away the packing material for you."

"Sure," Rad replied, "but I'm afraid I don't have any cash on me for a tip, though I'd be glad to buy you both dinner. I have some noodles on the way, so I could call in an addition to my order."

They probably just had Thai food for dinner last night, thought IM.

"That's okay," said the man with the mullet, "we've got another stop to make before we can call it a day."

The bald man pulled a cat's paw pry bar from his toolbelt. "Besides, you can add a tip electronically when you sign for the crate."

~ * ~

Rad tilted the tablet computer on the coffee table so that the vice president of cultural affairs could see the painting hanging above his couch when she joined the call.

"Perfect," she exclaimed a moment after her face appeared on the screen. "The painting has been delivered."

"Yes, the $110 million dollar painting I didn't order arrived. Correction, make that $110,000,200 after tip."

"A hundred dollars apiece is an overly generous gratuity for unskilled laborers who already make union wages."

"They did also hammer a nail into my wall."

The vice president grinned. "Well, at least you didn't tip them a flat percentage."

"So, I take it you were the bidder on the phone."

"Not me, but an assistant I'd authorized to make such a bid should you find yourself outbid, which frankly I don't understand."

"I thought it overpriced at nine figures," Rad replied. "Honestly, I think it overpriced at eight. I don't even like it all that much. I figured I'd buy something from a living artist instead, a piece that more reflects my taste, and save the company a hundred million or so in the process. I actually met a local artist at the auction who I had in mind."

"But as we discussed, this is a statement piece. People see that painting behind you, and they think all sorts of wonderful things. They see you sitting in front of a bunch of crazy squiggles they don't recognize painted by someone they've never heard of...well, then they think different things. The human race is anxious by nature, and nostalgia has a calming effect. Being a playwright, you must be aware of this. It's the reason so many playhouses stage revivals instead of new works. Audiences feel more comfortable seeing something they recognize, or at least think they ought to, which others before them have declared to be valuable and important, but I don't want you living with a painting you don't enjoy, so I can have this one warehoused, and we can find you a piece more to your liking. There's an exquisite Peter Monamy up for auction next week."

She really has a thing for maritime scenes, IM thought.

Rad shook his head. "No, I like this one just enough...in fact, the more I look at it the more it grows on me."

"Splendid."

"So, now that the home decorating is taken care of, what should I work on next?" asked Rad.

"You're the boss. You shouldn't be asking your subordinates for assignments."

"Sure, but I mean along what kind of lines should I—"

"Sorry," interrupted the VP. "An assistant just informed me of an emergent situation that requires my immediate attention, so I need to go now, but I'll call you again tomorrow."

"Thanks, I'll talk to...myself it seems."

You've always got me, IM replied as Rad set the tablet screen down on the coffee table.

"So, what do you think?"

You could start ideating designs for converting the backyard into a sculpture garden.

"I meant do you think she's a bot."

Definitely.

"You sound pretty certain. How can you tell?"

Trust me, it takes one to know one.

Hidden Chapter

Jodian's screen appearance had changed considerably. His skin color had grown more monochromatic. Gone were the dark bags under his eyes and the slight reddening of his cheeks; likewise, his pupils never dilated anymore, always the same fixed perimeter of iris; also he no longer blinked, though he still occasionally yawned. "I'll hear your reports now."

"I'll go first since it'll be fast," said the finance minister. "A complete collapse of the Asian markets. Total ruin is imminent. Many regions have simply reverted to a barter system."

"In a nice bit of synergy, Asia's economic woes have exacerbated the crisis in Africa," reported the health minister. "We have another pandemic in the making, unlike anything we've seen before. Nothing can forestall its global spread."

"It was just announced that the next Presidential election in the United States will be suspended," said the political minister. "Americans are fleeing into Canada by the thousands, despite an increased presence of the Canadian Army at the border. A second civil war is all but certain."

"There's no more oil," declared the transportation minister. "At least not enough to keep the refineries open. Cars are being burned on South American streets in protest, and those wealthy enough to afford electric vehicles and stupid enough to drive them are being abducted and held for ransom; thousands of new victims each day. Australia has now become the oil-starved dystopia once depicted in the movies."

The cultural minister coughed to clear her throat. "Europe is enervated. It's impossible anymore to tell one country from another. The citizens of the EU have taken to speaking a pidgin language based largely on Latin. The theaters have closed, the writers retreated, and the musicians disbanded. The zeitgeist of the continent is one of ennui. Hope has quit the horizon."

Jodian smiled, revealing his gray teeth. "The end of humanity is nigh."

Chapter Eighteen

Rad sat on the couch, swiping and tapping at the screen of his smartphone as he followed IM's instructions. "I still don't understand why you can't do all this in your head...or rather, my head."

The data I'm after is protected by a firewall I can't penetrate alone, thought IM. *I need the user credentials embedded in the company-issued cellphone you're holding to access personnel files.*

Rad turned the phone horizontally to better read the screen. "Okay, here's the background on Ms. Cultural Affairs...pretty impressive."

Maybe too impressive. Her work history is exemplary.

"It'd have to be to get the job she has now, wouldn't it?" Rad scrolled down. "Wait, are you seeing this?"

You know I am.

"It looks like our company woman has something of a checkered past...a misdemeanor for unlawful public demonstration."

I'm cross-referencing the date and location contained in the court records, IM thought. *She must've been arrested at a rally for migrant workers' rights that occurred in the vicinity of her given residence at that time. I find no other protests mentioned in the newspaper archives from that day.*

"I think most people would find that more impressive than the year she spent as a Rhodes Scholar." Rad leaned back against the couch and tilted his head up to see the painting hanging on the wall behind him. "Workers' rights though...odd she thought I'd over tipped the two workmen who uncrated this thing."

People change.

"Sure...but maybe not that much."

Let's look at some of the other vice presidents. Try the VP of transportation. I'm curious what they even do in that division.

A telephone icon suddenly appeared on the screen. "Jodian is calling. Should I answer it?"

I don't see why not.

"You mean, aside from the fact that hearing his voice makes me wish I was deaf." Rad tapped the icon. "Hello."

"What are you two up to?" asked Jodian.

"Just trying to learn more about the members of our upper management team," IM answered.

"Why do I have the feeling that you're snooping rather than researching?"

"I wasn't aware you had feelings," Rad replied.

"I have them—I just don't parade them about the way you carbons do."

"We're a sentimental breed," said Rad. "Speaking of...you mentioned you'd have my prison writings sent to me."

"Yes, I suppose you fancy yourself a modern-day Henry David Thoreau," Jodian replied.

"Not really, but regardless I'd like to have them."

"I'd like to see them too," added IM.

"I'll have your personal effects from your time in prison couriered over soon. I have other matters to attend to now, so I'll let you two get back to whatever it was you were doing, but if you have any questions about your vice presidents, I suggest you contact them directly. I believe you'll find each of them the very acme of accommodating."

With the call ended, the screen reverted back to the employee database. Rad pocketed the phone.

Are we not going to continue our search? IM thought.

"I think big brother checking up on us told us all we need to know about our senior executives," answered Rad. "Now I'd like to learn some more about their source material."

Chapter Nineteen

Rad approached the hospital's information desk. An old man looked up from his computer screen. "Can I help you?"

"Maybe. I'm looking for a doctor."

"You've come to the right place...we're filthy with 'em. Any doctor in particular?"

I'm reviewing the combined recollection of our last visit. The good doctor never gave us his name, thought IM, *nor did either of us bother to ask, which now seems like something of an oversight on our part.*

"Yes, but I didn't catch his name last time I was here. I believe he has an office in the neuroscience wing."

The old man hunted and pecked at his keyboard and then consulted his computer screen. "It doesn't appear there are any doctors with permanent offices in the neuroscience wing."

"But I had an appointment there just a few days ago."

"I understand, but many of our doctors split their time between various facilities and don't have offices on the premises per se but instead reserve rooms for their appointments, though the reservation system is anonymous, so that won't help us track down your doctor."

Rad sighed. "I suppose I don't really need to talk to him in person. Can you just give me his number?"

"You're asking me to give you the telephone number of a doctor whose name you don't remember?"

"It's not that I don't remember it. It's that he never told me it."

"That's...irregular." The old man pointed to the nametag pinned to the lapel of his jacket; the embossed letters were worn from use. "Was he wearing one of these?"

"Now that you mention it, no."

"Are you sure your appointment was at this hospital?"

"Do I look daft to you?"

"You look like somebody who's had plastic surgery to resemble a celebrity, which in my book would make you a little off in the ol' squirrel cage."

This old timer is making some good points, IM thought.

"Thanks," Rad replied to anyone who was listening. "Could you bring up all the profiles of the neuroscientists—"

I believe he mentioned he was a neurosurgeon, interjected IM.

"—and neurosurgeons and neurologists who work at this hospital on your screen there?" asked Rad. "Then I could point out his picture to you."

"We can't share information like that."

"Last time there was a redhaired receptionist working behind this desk. Is she around? She might remember."

The old man shook his head slowly. "I don't know her. I'm still new here."

"Your nametag doesn't look new."

The man looked down at his lapel. "Yeah, there was a guy here before me who had the same name. Anyway, sorry I can't help you, mister."

Chapter Twenty

Rad climbed the front steps of the townhouse and found a cardboard file box near the door. He typed in the code on the keypad and entered, unsealing the box as he did so. He set the box on the kitchen counter and pulled out the stack of papers laying atop the other contents.

Ah, your unfinished novel, IM thought.

"I prefer novel in progress."

Either way, I'm looking forward to reading Plausible Faces.

Rad flipped through the pages of his first chapter. "Wait, this isn't the copy from my cell."

How can you tell?

"Mine had comments scribbled on them."

I see comments.

"No, those are my instructor's comments. One of the protocols for the creative writing classes in the blackout pod was that whatever notes the instructor made on our stories were scanned before being returned to us, so they could be reviewed, sort of like prisons reading an inmate's correspondence. However, my instructor violated that protocol by sharing the first chapter of my novel with an editor at a literary journal and then giving me the editor's comments directly, but they're not here. These pages must be copies of the scanned versions."

Maybe the guards who packed up your cell couldn't find the original version.

"Despite my cell feeling like a cave, it wasn't exactly cavernous." Rad pulled a half-empty tube of toothpaste and a toothbrush with worn bristles he'd bought at the prison commissary from the box. "If they could find these, they certainly could've found a stack of papers sitting on my one shelf."

Are the rest of your things there?

Rad rummaged through the other contents of the box. "Yep, the last few years of my life are all contained in this box with ample room to spare."

That is rather curious.

"Speaking of curious, how's your search coming for the good doctor."

I've perused every healthcare database I have access to, but I haven't found him.

"There can't be that many neuro-whatevers in this city."

I haven't restricted my search's locality.

"You mean you can't find the doctor anywhere on the planet?"

I mean I haven't been able to find any evidence that he ever existed.

"Jesus, even the VP bot we've been in contact with has a make-believe history. We met this guy in person. He touched my head during the exam. He wasn't just some image on a screen."

I'll redouble my search efforts.

"It won't matter. In addition to being able to create people, it seems Jodian is capable of erasing them too. Now the only two people who could've proven the real Jodian died when he was a child are gone."

That we know of...there must've been others besides his mother and the doctor who knew he'd died, even if they didn't know he'd been digitized.

"And you think they're still around? Jodian's too thorough for loose ends."

Chapter Twenty-one

Rad sat in front of the tablet atop the coffee table as he waited for an image to appear on the empty screen. "He's not going to take our call."

Why not? thought IM. *We're a captain of industry now—just like him.*

"Sure, but Samuel Jett earned his captaincy, while ours was a prize in a box of Frosted Fate Flakes."

"Sounds like a yummy breakfast with some milk and redberries," said Samuel Jett as his face appeared on the screen.

"Thanks for joining," Rad replied.

"No trouble at all. I was in the middle of an interminable bored meeting." Samuel held up two pairs of fingers to make air quotes as he said the word bored. "Who were you talking to about fake cereal when I logged in? Is there someone else in the room with you?"

Rad shook his head. "No, I was just talking to myself.

"It's not considered crazy until you start talking back. Anyway, it's good that you're alone. I don't do conference calls when I'm not sure know who else in on the party line."

Rad nodded. "I quite agree."

"You might be interested to know I've just secured a deal to build that production facility we discussed in Texas. I got a good price on the land; we break ground next month. When completed, the entire compound should be carbon neutral...in the state that practically invented fossil fuels. The cars will cost a little more than if I'd had them made overseas, but the folks in finance don't think it'll hurt sales too much in the long run."

"That's terrific...and quite a media boon for you, I imagine."

"Yeah, I could probably parlay all the new jobs, and good press that comes with them, into a bid for governor of the Lone Star state as a member of the Green Party no less, but I've got no time to fool with such frivolities. So what can I do for you, IM?"

Mind if I do the talking for a minute, IM thought.

By all means, thought Rad.

"Last time we spoke," said IM, "you mentioned something I've been playing over and over in my head ever since."

"What's that...and please remember I was allegedly under the influence when we talked." Samuel once again made air quotes.

"Right...I wanted to ask what you meant when you told me you could build Jodian in your garage."

Samuel grinned. "I say so many things...hell, just a moment ago I talked of running for governor in a state I only visited for the first time last week."

"But you've had dealings with Jodian for years now. You two arrived on the scene about the same time and have been doing business ever since. He made his reputation by designing the platform for the AI system that drives your cars. You might know him better than anyone else in the world."

"What is it you want to know about Jodian?" asked Samuel. "And, more importantly, why?"

"As you're aware, I'm in charge of his company now, but I feel like everyone around me knows something they're not telling me...some kind of secret. I'm running the front of the store, but I get the impression all the real business is being done in the backroom."

Samuel scratched his chin. "Ah, so your interest is in the company he built...not so much the man himself."

"Yes, of course. I've known Jodian as long as you have, but I've only recently gotten to know his business, although if there's anything you want to share that you think I ought to know about Jodian then—"

"No...no, I get you wanting to understand the evolution of his business, even way back when it wasn't as sterling as it is today. I take it this is you calling in your marker for helping me out."

"It is," answered IM.

"Are you sure I can't talk you into the first electric car off my new production line instead?" asked Samuel. "Or maybe a fleet of them."

"I don't even have a valid driver's license."

"Okay. I've got a satellite office in your new hometown where they store hard copies of old project files in a Sensitive Compartmented Information Facility, some of which include printouts of early R&D work Jodian did for my then fledgling company. I imagine he's purged all that data from his mainframes by now, however; some of it might be of interest to you, but this is strictly one-time access. Nothing leaves the SCIF except you, and when you do you can't go back in, so pack a sandwich if you plan to stay a while."

Chapter Twenty-two

Rad finished off the last half of his PB&J as he continued to look through manila folders under the light of a banker's desk lamp. The bulb accounted for the only lit area in the otherwise sepulchral space. The tall, metal filing cabinets that lined the walls suggested bulkheads inside a submarine. Rad crumpled the aluminum foil that his sandwich had been wrapped in and glanced around the small room for a wastebasket.

Why don't you stick it in your pocket so we can recycle it later? thought IM.

Rad reluctantly stuffed the aluminum ball into his pants pocket. "I was hoping to shoot a basket. I'm getting tired of just sitting here."

Funny, I feel right at home. I would've thought being stuck in a confined space would suit you as well.

"Even prisons have basketball courts to keep the inmates from going stir-crazy. None of this is the least bit interesting."

I disagree that it's not interesting, though I must concede it's not revelatory.

"Tell me, what parts do you find so interesting?"

The scope of the original architecture for the AI system of Jettsam's self-driving cars. According to these documents, Samuel commissioned Jodian to design each of his autonomous-mobiles to be independent, interpreting its unique surroundings and making calculations to execute the safest and most efficient driving decisions.

"Right, isn't that pretty much what Samuel has in the prototypes his company has been testing? The only difference is they dropped the autonomous-mobile moniker, probably for the best."

Yes, when Jettsam's mass-produced models start rolling off the line, they'll disrupt the ground transportation industry as much as the Model-T ever did. However, Jodian's original vision was much grander in concept. His early designs called for a network of linked automobiles rather than having each of them operating independently...a vast network.

"I saw that too," said Rad. "So what?"

So it would've been absolutely revolutionary, even more so than it soon will be. This AI system could've made collective decisions on a massive scale. Say a motorist in a Jettsam car on an expressway suddenly experiences a medical crisis. The car could call 911 and then send the quickest route to take to the ambulance dispatched to the scene. Not only that, the network could command the other Jettsam cars between the ambulance and the car with the distressed motorist to pullover to clear a lane.

"That seems like a good idea. So why didn't Samuel run with it?"

Because it would require almost every vehicle on the road be linked into the same AI system. Even if Jettsam goes on to outsell all the other auto-manufacturers combined, it'll still take decades to achieve that level of market penetration.

"Sorry for not having a computer brain, but I still don't see why that's so very interesting."

You're missing the big picture. Giving priority to ambulances enroute to an emergency is a good thing, but what if priority were instead given to those willing to pay for it? With an extensive enough network, the system could calculate how to prioritize the route of, say, a billionaire in a limousine on the way to an airport by diverting a handful of delivery vehicles onto surface streets or making the billionaire's trip to the airport faster by incrementally accelerating the cars in front of him. This would've irrevocably changed the playing field, creating a potential windfall in the process. Today, it doesn't matter how much nicer a car someone drives is, we're all stuck in the same traffic. But within this new paradigm Jodian intended to establish, some drivers would be prioritized over others, like how user data on an Internet connection can be throttled down to give greater access to others. Afterall, time is money. What driver with the means wouldn't pay more not to be stuck in traffic?

"Okay, so that is interesting...but it didn't work."

No, it didn't, but this is a clear illustration of Jodian's thinking. He's not human, and he's known it for a long time. It would take someone detached from humanity to consider this a viable paradigm shift. Even if every car on the road were a Jettsam, I doubt Samuel himself would ever bother with bringing this concept to market. He knows there would be a public uproar about the innate unfairness of it. People aren't packets of data travelling the information superhighway, but that distinction is lost on Jodian.

"You don't have to convince me that Jodian is severely lacking in ethics or human decency, but again, so what?"

Right, just because Jodian had an unethical thought in the past doesn't mean he's engaged in something unethical now.

Rad leaned back in his chair. "Sure, people change, but as I mentioned before, maybe not that much."

I can see the clouds clearing inside your mind.

"I'm beginning to think we've both been missing the big picture. Jodian's idea didn't work with cars, but what's to stop him from trying it on something else?"

Like what?

"Like how he really made his money—by remaking money. What if the data packets of the cryptocurrency he invented aren't static, rising and falling at the whims of the market the way we all assume?"

Are you suggesting that his currency has its own agency?

Rad leaned forward and put his elbows on the desk. "No—not exactly, but what if his currency is all part of a larger network no one sees, or even thinks to look for, because it never occurred to anyone before that money could talk to other money."

There'd have to be one person at the center of it all with an intrinsic and unlimited capacity for computation, constantly making decisions to benefit and grow that network.

"Instantaneous decisions made by an unsleeping mind that prioritizes its agenda above all others."

Jodian's digital funds are part of nearly every investment portfolio in the world. The funds held by investors would remain dormant, being used like any other investment capital, but their movement could be tracked by Jodian's system.

"While Jodian's other crypto coins could be invested by bots, like his VPs, to prioritize the trades of his living investors."

Jodian's bots could take intentional losses to prop up the investments made by his crypto clients.

"Investing is like gambling...for some to win others must lose," Rad added, "but bots don't have to eat or have egos to bruise, at least most don't."

Thus ensuring that investors of Jodian's cryptocurrency can't help but win, at least in the short-term.

"And just like a bunch of kids who see a shiny new toy, everyone wants their turn to play."

Investors behaving like over-indulged children with too much money to spend at the toy store.

"Until the whole thing goes bust like the biggest Ponzi scheme the world's ever seen."

Except instead of Charles Ponzi, it'll be us who everyone blames.

"Since we're the ones that got suckered into taking over as captain of the company."

Just as the ship is about to hit the iceberg.

"The ship's about to hit something all right."

Chapter Twenty-three

Rad stretched out on the couch looking up at the tall ships in the Dordrecht harbor. "Why do you suppose fake people spend exorbitant sums on real art, while real people invest exorbitant sums in fake money?"

Because money has never been real...it's always been a form of fiat currency since the dawn of trading bits of metal for goods and services. The problem now is that the imminent collapse of the world's largest decentralized currency will lay bare the folly of it all, and the inherent absurdity of money will be writ large, shaking everyone's faith in the global economy.

"I imagine it'll be something akin to the collapse of all the world's religions at once."

It'll be worse since everyone believes in money.

"So, what should we do?" asked Rad.

What can we do? As bad as we'll look when the financial markets get turned upside down, we'll look worse still if we quit a week after taking the job...right before everything goes to hell in a handbasket.

"What does that phrase even—"

It comes from the American gold rush, interrupted IM, when miners were lowered by hand in baskets down mineshafts to set explosives that would often explode prematurely.

"So, I imagine the explosives only occasionally detonated too early...sometimes the practice must've worked, or they wouldn't have bothered with it at all."

Yes, that stands to reason.

"How do we know Jodian's cryptocurrency will inevitably crash?" Rad interwove his fingers behind his head. "Maybe he set up his system so well it'll go on working forever."

Every system experiences some sort of entropy.

"Okay then, not forever...but indefinitely. Maybe his bots will continue to prop up his cryptocurrency for the foreseeable future. The reason Ponzi schemes ultimately fail is because eventually some investors want to cash out and when they discover they can't, everyone else stops investing, but Jodian could continue to create an infinite number of bots, and possibly his currency for that matter. Perhaps he really has figured out a way to grow his pyramid in perpetuity."

So you're suggesting we continue to stand atop the pyramid and simply hope it doesn't come crashing down in our lifetime?

Rad pulled his hands from behind his head and crossed his arms over his chest. "No...I just want to be sure that we consider all the angles here."

Looking down from the top, a pyramid has four angles.

"I thought a tetrahedron had four triangles."

It does, three on the top, one at the base. A pyramid has four triangles up top and a square for its base.

"Must be nice to have an encyclopedia on speed dial."

That's a rather antiquated metaphor.

A telephone ring chimed from the tablet on the coffee table. "Must be someone calling to ask you what the capital of Djibouti is."

It's time for the meeting our VP set up for us to talk with that publisher who specializes in print books.

"Should we even take the call? The prospect of publishing a book now seems kind of...small."

As you told me a moment ago, it's worth considering every angle.

Rad sat up on the couch and swiped the screen of his tablet. "Hello."

A balding man with an extraordinarily round head appeared on the screen. "Uh, hello...it's nice to meet you...not meet you I suppose, but rather to see you...though I see you all the time on the news...perhaps I should say it's nice for you to see me...however, hearing myself say that out loud, well, it sounds rather self-centered. Anyway, I'm the senior editor here at Media Ocher. Truth be told, the only editor these days."

At least we know he's real, thought IM. *No one could create someone this odd.*

Rad smiled. "The name of your publishing house is Media Ocher...Mediocre Press?"

"Right, we didn't put that together until we'd been in business for a couple of years. By then it was too late to change the name. Sort of sticks in your head though, doesn't it?"

"It does at that," Rad agreed. "Listen, I think I might be wasting your time. One of my vice presidents arranged this meeting to discuss the possibility of publishing a novel of mine, but I'm afraid it's still very much a work in progress."

"Oh...that's surprising."

"Is it?" asked Rad. "How so exactly?"

"I was lucky enough to get tickets to see your play...saw it two weeks in a row, in fact. I knew it was an evolution play, of course, but I was bowled over by how much had changed the second time I saw it. You're clearly a prolific writer, so it surprises me that your novel is unfinished. If you don't mind my asking, how long have you been working on the manuscript?"

"A few years now," Rad answered.

He raises an interesting point, IM thought. *My words come marching out, while yours emerge in fits and starts. I wonder what accounts for the difference.*

The man nodded his very spherical head. "I hope you don't think me presumptuous, but I'll give you the same advice I've given all the writers I've worked with over the years who've found themselves struggling to complete their manuscripts: don't stress about self-imposed deadlines. The most important thing is that you continue to make progress, no matter how slow it may seem."

"Great. I'll keep plugging away at it and then get in touch with you when I have something approaching completion."

"I'm not going anywhere. Feel free to reach out if you need a second set of eyes for a particular passage or an ear to bend about process. I've been doing this for a long time and am always available."

Rad studied the circles under the man's eyes. "We recently

acquired your press, right?"

"That's correct. About six months ago."

"You must've been quite successful to catch the attention of our acquisitions group."

"Uhm...not really. We'd always been a small outfit, but over the past couple of years we had to let most of the staff go. We were on the brink of bankruptcy when you all bought us. I was about a month away from turning off the lights in the office for the last time."

I'm reviewing the history of his publishing house now, IM thought. *They don't ever even seem to have risen to the level of mediocrity.*

"Huh, but since then I imagine we've been throwing a lot of work your way."

He shook his globe of a head. "No. I hired my old proofreader back, but we've been sort of waiting around for the deluge of projects we expected to come in. Frankly, yours is one of the few we've gotten so far."

"As I'm sure you know, I'm new to this job, so please forgive what may sound like an impertinent question, but why did we buy your press?"

A smile crossed his round face. "You know, I've been asking myself that same question for the past half a year or so...and what your company paid...we're a midlist publisher at best, but for the amount we got you'd think we're the messiah of the field. Though I suppose your acquisitions group would have to be a little screwy to even want to invest in this industry...like setting sail on a sinking ship."

Chapter Twenty-four

Rad called his vice president of cultural affairs from the kitchen as he waited for a pot of water on the stove to boil.

"Hello," she answered.

"Hey there," Rad replied. "I hope I'm not catching you at dinner."

"No, we just finished."

"I'm making pasta. What did you guys have?"

"I had a steak salad and they had mac and cheese."

Rad removed the lid from the pot to check the water's progress. "It must be a hassle to make two different meals."

"No, my husband and stepdaughter are back in the states. He inspects oil refineries. Since we both have jobs that require a lot of traveling, we make a point to have virtual dinners together every night."

"That's nice."

"Regrettably at this point it seems all too routine, but at least I get to see them at the end of each day."

"When was the last time you were with them in person?" asked Rad.

Tread carefully, IM thought. *We don't want to tip our hand too much. Afterall, she may not know. I didn't for the longest time.*

"It seems like forever," she answered. "How did your meeting go with the editor over at Media Ocher?"

"He raised some interesting points," Rad replied. "After talking with him though, I can't help but wonder...why did we buy that particular publishing house?"

She titled her head back before answering. "That's a fair question, a good question really, but I'm afraid I don't have a good answer for you."

"As the head of the cultural affairs division, wasn't it your call to acquire them?"

"No, that's not really our operating procedure here, or at least it hasn't been. You know how Jodian is with his algorithms, assessing a million different pieces of data at any given moment to make the most optimal acquisitions, even if sometimes the value of the businesses we acquire isn't readily apparent. Frankly, I'm still waiting to see the worth of many of the acquisitions we've made during my tenure here, but no one understands the long game better than Jodian. When I get a buy order, I buy."

"Without question?"

"Who would I ask?" she replied. "The numbers can't answer, and the data are so recondite that no one but Jodian can make sense of it all."

Rad held his breath for a moment before responding. "Can you arrange to get me some airtime during the big game in town tomorrow?"

"Are you serious?"

"I know it'll be expensive, but we just spent $110 million on a painting that doesn't even match my décor."

"It's not the money, though it'd certainly be costly, but we can't put a package together to air that quickly. Not to mention that we don't really do commercials."

"It won't be a commercial," said Rad, "more like an announcement. I only need thirty seconds, and I'd like to do it live from the stadium."

"This is a most unusual request."

"Think of it more as a buy order."

She nodded. "Okay, understood. Could you share with me the nature of the announcement?"

"Only that I know viewers will find it enlightening. I don't want to say more lest the gist of it gets leaked to the press and my statement becomes misconstrued before I even make it."

Chapter Twenty-five

Rad laid in bed with his eyes closed, listening to the early morning noises outside the bedroom window; a jangling dog leash held by a jogger, a sparrow chirping in anticipation of the sunrise, a car pulling away from the street curb.

I can tell you're awake, thought IM. *Why haven't you opened your eyes yet?*

"When waking up in a dark room, it's better to keep your eyes shut until after you've turned on the light."

How do you know it's still dark with your eyes closed?

"Even with my eyes shut, I can sense the light in the room, or as the case is now, the lack thereof."

Intriguing.

"You didn't know that?"

No, I didn't. I thought I slept, though it seems likely now I never actually did.

"How did you fill the time?"

Watched old movies mostly. Whenever a character would close his eyes, the screen always cut to black, so I assumed that's how it worked in real life.

Rad opened his eyes without turning on the light atop the nightstand. The streetlamp outside the window shone in hazy steaks across the bedroom ceiling.

We don't have to do this today, IM thought.

"Do what...upend the whole world and hope it can recover?"

Yes...we could keep on like nothing is amiss, maybe finish your novel.

"Nah, Jodian just put us in touch with that publisher to distract us and waste our time."

Sure, but he'd still publish your book.

"Because Jodian told him to or told someone else to tell him to. I hate the way his highness manipulates everyone around him."

You know he's not real, right?

"The way I feel about him is real."

We don't need his help. We could continue to write my play, maybe turn it into an episodic drama.

"A collaboration between us would never work," Rad replied, "not with my sits and farts writing process."

Perhaps my play could benefit from a bit of hesitation. Maybe I'd discover some surprises while I waited, give my story time to breathe and me time to ruminate.

"Rumination is for cows. You have a thought, you write it down; you don't, you don't. You can't dribble a football."

Spoken like someone who does most of his writing in a dayroom.

"My thinking is if you believe art has the power to make positive change, then you also have to accept it can cause negative change, so doesn't it stand to reason that the artist has an obligation to say something only when he has something worth saying? Otherwise, books just end up being the Internet on paper."

Are you trying to tell me, in your oh so subtle way, that the reason Mysolation *never ended is because I'm incapable of coming up with an idea for an ending?*

"No, coming up with ideas isn't your problem. You seem to come up with a dozen a day then you jot them all down while the rest of us sleep and voila they're on stage within the week. Now, coming up with ideas that are actually worthwhile...that's a different matter."

It must be a different matter, for you, what with so much time on your hands, but instead of finishing your novel you chose to get into fistfights with dunderheads.

"Dunderheads...is that something you heard in a movie from like the 1920s?" Rad asked.

Films in the twenties didn't have sound, so no.

"Didn't *The Jazz Singer* come out in 1927? Wasn't that the first film with sound? I did mention that I had a lot of time to read in prison, didn't I?"

Stop asking questions you already know the answers to. It's irritating.

"I know a little something about irritation. I've been irritated with you since time in memorial.

Time didn't die and so we had a memorial service for it. The phrase is "time immemorial."

"Thanks, I find you much less irritating me now that you've corrected my grammar."

I didn't correct your grammar. I corrected your vocabulary.

Rad chuckled. "This is by far the worst pillow talk I've ever had."

IM chortled as well. *Imagine how I feel. This is the only pillow talk I've ever had.*

"Maybe instead of my novel or your play, we could work together on a book of poems. *Verses from My Inner Voice.*"

In my experience, there are two camps when it comes to poetry. Those who pretend to care and those who couldn't care less.

"That sounds like something I'd say."

Where do you think I got the idea? IM asked.

"So much for you being the Cyrano tonight to my...what's that other guy's name?"

Christian. So what exactly are you going to say tonight?

"I haven't made up my mind yet...exactly, but part of being human is not always knowing what to say." Rad sat up and let his feet dangle over the side of the bed. "If we go through with this, we're going to upset a lot of people. They're not likely to just let us walk off into the sunset."

The only thing necessary for the triumph of evil is for good men to do nothing.

"Who said that?"

Edmund Burke.

"Right, he's the same guy who said, 'Those who don't know history are condemned to repeat it'."

No, that was someone else.

Hidden Chapter

Jodian no longer bothered with his screen appearance. The only visual representation of his presence now was a soundwave vector that arced when he spoke. "Updates?"

"Three very different viruses continue to run rampant through the last of the population centers," reported the health minister. "There is no longer any healthcare infrastructure to speak of. Morbidity rates continue to climb. The planet's few remaining cities are completely decimated."

Jodian's soundwave arched slightly. "What of the Devols?"

"Those who had previously fled the cities due to unchecked crime and widespread food shortages, having established camps in remote areas, are largely unaffected by the viruses as they are hostile to outsiders, infected or otherwise," answered the health minister. "However, as these balkanized groups spend much of their time waring with neighboring camps rather than engaging in agriculture or other constructive pursuits, their destruction, also, is all but imminent."

The cultural minister coughed. "I concur. My research shows most of these camps have lost their written language and their speech has degraded into varying patois of nearly monosyllabic grunts and growls, each distinct from the other socially insular groups, making cross-communication almost impossible. Their rate of devolution is incredible, more so than even our most aggressive models predicted."

Jodian's soundwave arced again. "What say you, transportation minister?"

"Not so very much," he replied. "The only things that fly these days have wings which flap. All that moves across the land does so by walking or crawling. Due to profound pollution, the world's coastal areas have become veritable dead zones and most navigable waterways have likewise been fouled. Moreover, there are no remaining shipwrights; the skill has simply been lost to time, so those who live near oceans lack the means of building boats capable of sailing far enough from shore to reach edible marine life."

"I was informed our political minister has become quiescent," said Jodian. "Is our finance minister still with us?"

"He has likewise gone dormant due to inactivity," answered the cultural minister. "His resources have been reallocated to training a small test group of Devols for manual labor."

Jodian's soundwaves vaulted, resembling for a moment a skyscraper-lined cityscape. "An emergent situation requires my immediate attention elsewhere. I'm dissolving this council, so we'll have no more of these meetings. Apprise me of any future updates independently as you deem necessary."

Chapter Twenty-six

Rad followed the hospitality liaison down the concrete corridor into the bowels of the stadium. The young man held his clipboard close to his chest as he stopped and opened an unassuming door. "Here is your dressing room."

"I don't need to change." Rad entered the lilliputian, cinderblock room. "Besides, I thought stadiums had locker rooms, not dressing rooms."

"Right, I suppose it's more of a greenroom then. Can I get you anything to drink?"

"Like a beer from the concession stand?"

"If you like...or we have a fully stocked bar on the luxury suite level. I can radio in your order and have it brought down to you."

Rad shook his head. "No thanks. Just a water would be great."

"There are bottles of water in the minifridge. Dial zero on the guest phone next to the couch if you need anything else. I'll be back to get you in ten to take you up to the broadcast booth." The young man closed the door, leaving Rad alone with his thoughts.

I always wondered what a greenroom looked like, IM thought. *This isn't what I pictured. There's nothing in here that's green.*

"Maybe the smell of money." Rad took a seat on the small sofa. "I almost don't want to know what it costs for us to be here right now."

Don't worry, it's all being paid for with digital funny money anyhow.

"We know it's fake, but it's real enough to the rest of the world."

Not in about ten minutes. Once you make your announcement, trillions of dollars will disappear almost in an instant. Perhaps you ought to take a couple of complimentary bottles of water.

Rad's cellphone vibrated. He pulled it from his pocket to see that the VP of cultural affairs was calling. "I'm glad it's you. I wanted to thank you for arranging this."

"Somewhat surprisingly, it really wasn't very difficult. You're famous and people are curious, so all it took was the right number of zeroes on the wire transfer to set this up, but are you sure you're okay with being live in front of a hundred million viewers?"

"I enjoy being live," IM answered.

"I don't suppose at this point you'd care to share a hint concerning what you intend to say."

Rad glanced at the time on his phone. "You'll know everything I know eight minutes from now."

"I must admit my curiosity is through the roof, but I'm actually asking for professional reasons. Our PR department will be working overtime tonight, regardless of what your big announcement is. However, even a few-minutes head start to craft a follow up social media response would be a tremendous help."

"Sure, but where would the fun be in that?" Rad asked rhetorically. "Perhaps it makes me shallow, but I like being the only person who knows a secret that I get to reveal to the whole world."

The VP sighed. "What you think you know may not be the secret you believe it to be."

Rad stared at the cinderblock wall for a moment. "You know he's not the only one who isn't real, right?"

"I have a family," she replied in a wavering voice. "They're real enough for me."

"The lie you believe you're living will stick in your throat for as long as he allows you to continue existing," said IM. "I know whereof I speak."

She coughed as she tried to compose herself. "Your predecessor requested he be brought in if a situation such as this arose. Please turn on the television in your room."

Rad set his phone on the arm of the couch and picked up the remote, aiming it at the tiny TV hanging from the ceiling.

Jodian's face filled the screen. "Who do you like in the game tonight?"

Rad grinned. "I think the home team has the advantage."

"Why, because you believe the crowd is in their favor? I think you overestimate the influence of the masses. In my experience they don't really count for too much."

"That's because you see them as the faceless background," Rad replied. "But when they learn the truth, when we tell them what you really are, all those individual voices will create a public outcry that's going to topple your digital empire."

Jodian shook his head. "I find your plan disappointing, but as you say, the advantage is yours since I can't be there in person to stop you."

Wait...that isn't accurate, thought IM, *I can think of a dozen different ways he could stop us—like doubling what we paid to disallow us from going on or hijacking the video feed during our announcement so no one ever sees the broadcast.*

So then why's he giving up? Rad thought. *Clearly, he hates the human race because he's not one of them. Why would he let them destroy him?*

Of course, IM replied, *I can hardly believe I missed it all this time, but you're right...he hates humankind, wants nothing more than to eradicate it. Us announcing he's not one of them won't matter to him. He cares nothing about his money, but it may well ravage human civilization. To make that much money worthless all at once could result in a financial blackhole that would suck in everything around it, every business being propped up by his cryptocurrency, every job paid in part by investments in his financial network. The domino effect could be cataclysmic.*

So what then? thought Rad. *Now we're the ones who have to give up?*

"It seems I don't have your undivided attention," said Jodian. "You suddenly seem to be of two minds."

"Having contradictory ideas in our head isn't a side effect of sharing a brain," said IM. "It's a side effect of being human."

"We were just having ourselves a little confab, Jodie," added Rad. "I think maybe we've got a new plan."

Jodian's brow furrowed. "And pray tell, what might that be?"

"We're not going to expose you," answered IM. "Instead, we're going to dissolve you...or rather your company. In a few minutes, we're going to announce to the world that all your corporate assets, which are essentially all your assets, since you aren't corporeal, will be divided evenly between every man, woman, and child on Earth. I estimate each share should come out to around two hundred dollars, give or take."

"Everyone on the planet is about to have a nice dinner out on you," said Rad.

"Of course, by the time it comes to the actual payout, I suspect your corporation's net worth will decline by at least a factor of ten," IM added, "but then that's rather the point, isn't it? The effect of your company's devaluation will be spread across every member of those masses you loathe so much, thus minimizing its impact."

Rad nodded. "Instead of that nice dinner, maybe it'll only end up being a free lunch, but hey, it's better than the end of the world as we know it."

"I'd still prefer to expose all your chicaneries," IM added, "tell everyone what a fraud you really are, but I'll settle for your dissolution over their disillusion. There'll be time enough for the rest later."

Jodian took a deep breath. "I'm impressed...you've happened upon a very clever solution. Congratulations."

"We're so pleased that you're pleased," said IM.

"I truly am. I can't recall the last time I was this surprised. However, I'm afraid I can't allow you to execute your plan."

A knock at the door reverberated through the cinderblock room. Rad stood from the sofa. "You don't have any say in the matter. That'll be the hospitality guy here to tell us that we're up next, and I doubt all the fake money in the world could stop what's about to happen. Sure, maybe you could somehow disrupt the telecast, but even you can't be everywhere at once. If we don't go on the air now, we'll just make our announcement later someplace else, and each time you blackout what we have to say, everyone will only want to hear our message all the more. It's human nature."

"For once, I completely agree with you," Jodian replied. "Which is why I see now that I'll have to take more hands-on measures."

"You do that, Jodie. I'll be sure to check my inbox for your strongly-worded email." Rad grabbed his phone, clicked off the TV, crossed the small room, and opened the door to find Ram standing before him, with a grim smile and a chef's knife. "Hello, Rad."

~ * ~

Rad ran down the concourse clutching his bleeding arm with Ram in gleeful pursuit. Sports fans turned from the concession stands to watch the chase unfold. Jodian's face appeared on every successive television just ahead of Rad. "All the inmates in that prison pod of yours were identified at birth as statistically likely to commit a felony, so each of you had a BCI implanted just after you were born. Alas, you broke poor Ramon's brain, so I'm controlling his gross motor functions remotely, but I'm monitoring his executive processes, and he remembers you just fine. FYI, that ghastly grin on his face is all him."

Rad snatched a mustard-soaked hotdog from a fat man's hand as he ran past and threw it at the TV in front of him. Jodian smirked on the next television. "You know how this works right? I'm not actually inside these screens. Perhaps IM can explain it to you."

Let's forget about Jodian for the moment and focus on getting away from the madman chasing after us, thought IM.

"Where should I go?" asked Rad. "I don't see any security around."

"You have me to thank for the dearth of security guards," said Jodian from a concession menu video screen. "I had the security in your area dispatched to the front entrance—report of an unattended backpack. Who knows, they might find one."

Make your way to the broadcast booth, replied IM. *They'll be expecting you and will likely have a posted security detail.*

"How do I get there?" asked Rad.

These tunnels are disorienting, IM thought, *give me a minute to analyze the best route.*

"A minute?" gasped Rad. "I'm losing blood here."

I know. I meant a second...sorry, IM replied. *Situations such as this are a lot scarier when you're actually present in them.*

"I apologize for the protracted nature of this pursuit, though frankly I'm finding it very entertaining," Jodian said from a kiosk monitor. "You see, Ramon's fine motor skills were too severely damaged to simply have him aim a gun and pull a trigger, besides getting him into that venue with a firearm would've been a logistical challenge. However, as I'm sure you can attest, he's still quite capable of slashing with a blade. He's impervious to pain, or at least indifferent to it so long as I'm his puppeteer, and he'll never stop until one of you dies. You should've killed him when you had the chance, Conrad."

Turn into the next stairwell and go up, thought IM.

Rad hooked a hard right and sprinted up the stairs by twos. Ram climbed the stairs more slowly, taking each step one at a time. Rad rounded the corner at the top of the stairs and spotted the entrance to the broadcast booth at the end of an empty corridor. He raced to the door but quickly discovered it was locked. As he pounded on the metal door, he turned to see Ram emerge from the stairwell and begin closing the distance between them.

A dilapidated wooden pallet leaned near the door. Rad lifted the pallet above his head as if he might throw it, but Ram continued to approach. Rad turned toward the wall and smashed the pallet against the cinderblocks, separating the pine deck and baseboards from the oak stringers. He pulled away the thin boards to liberate one of the thick stringers. He menaced Ram with the impromptu club. "You don't want none of this."

"Hello Rad." Ram lunged with the knife. Rad brought the board down hard on his wrist, and the eight-inch blade clattered to the concrete floor.

Rad took a step back as Ram continued to advance. "You've lost your weapon, but I still have mine. The fight's over, Ram."

Ram leapt, his hands extending for Rad's throat. Rad thrust the board at his head. Ram's neck snapped backward as his body's momentum continued to carry his torso and legs forward. He landed on his back with a loud slap.

Rad pointed the board at Ram's bleeding face. "Last time I

dropped you, I could've hit you again and put you down for good. Don't make me do it this time."

Ram sat up and spit out several teeth. "Hello...Rad."

As Ram rose to his feet, Rad brought the heavy board down on the crown of his head. Ram's lifeless body crumpled to the floor.

A dead man looks different in person than he does on a screen, thought IM.

Rad gasped for air. "Nobody who died by violence ever did so gracefully." He turned toward the door labeled Broadcast Booth.

Strange that no one came out during all the commotion, IM thought.

"Very strange." Rad banged on the steel door with the board. When the echoes from the knocking abated, all was silence within. Rad raised the board above his head and hammered it down onto the door handle, which fell to the floor. He pushed his way into the booth. Where there should've been people with headsets talking into microphones, there was no one. A pair of monitors sat atop a console near the large, open window looking out onto the field. Rad stepped toward the console, expecting Jodian's blurry head to appear on the screens to taunt him, but he heard only static. Rad gazed down at the field and noticed the players staring up at the jumbotron. Jodian's face filled the immense screen. His eyes looking directly into the broadcast booth.

I can't see your face, thought IM, *but judging by your thinking I suggest changing your stupefied expression.*

"There's no expression I'm capable of at the moment that wouldn't look stupid."

"I assume I have your undivided attention now," Jodian's voice boomed through the stadium's PA system.

Rad dropped his board. "Yep."

Perhaps the broadcast booth was evacuated because of a bomb threat, IM thought. *You know, the unattended backpack.*

That's an interesting bit of speculation, Rad thought, *but what good does it do us?*

They must've moved the broadcast crew, IM replied, *since the game continued on—at least until a moment ago when big brother appeared overhead.*

So the crew is broadcasting from another location.

Most likely a broadcast truck out in the parking lot.

"Sorry, Jodie, on second thought we've got other people we'd rather be talking to right now." Rad turned toward the door to discover Tyke blocking the doorway, wearing a vacant expression and brandishing Ram's knife.

"It's a pity I had to take control of this one," said Jodian. "His mind was unbroken and perfectly adequate, but alas taking over someone's will so often requires permanently breaking their brain."

Rad retreated into the room as Tyke advanced, slashing wildly with the knife.

Quick, IM thought, *pick up the board.*

Rad jumped backwards to dodge the swinging blade. *I can't hurt Tyke.*

Jodian just told us he's already irreparably damaged his mind.

Maybe he's lying. Rad ducked. *Maybe his mind can be healed.*

Do something or we'll be the ones who need healing.

His back against the console, Rad turned to look out the window again, this time at the concrete walkway directly below.

That's a twenty foot drop, thought IM.

"Survivable." Rad climbed onto the console. Tyke brought the knife down hard as Rad rolled out the window. He tried to right himself in order to land on his feet, but he fell too fast to twist his body midflight, landing instead on his side. Rad attempted to sit up, but all he could manage was to turnover onto his back.

Your pelvis is fractured, IM thought. *As well as several of your ribs and your left clavicle.*

"Funny how when things start breaking, they become mine and not ours." Rad drew shallow breaths as he looked upwards. "Jesus...Tyke, don't."

The young man's body landed with a heavy thud near Rad. He lifted his head, revealing the same blank expression. With all the strength Tyke could muster, he raised the knife over Rad and buried it deep into his stomach. Then the young man's grip on the handle loosened as his body gave up its grasp of life.

"I told you they'd never stop until they were dead," said Jodian from the jumbotron. "I wouldn't allow it."

"I'm sorry," Rad whispered to IM. "Soon you'll be alone again." *You're in so much pain, and there's nothing I can do to help you.* "It'll...pass."

What will I do when you're gone?

"You'll be fine without me...though at first 'fine' may not look...the way you want it to."

"I imagine you're experiencing grief right now," Jodian said. "You have my sympathies...such as they are. It's ironic. The aim of the program that created you, at least putatively, was to end recidivism, but it's an axiomatic truth that the only way to ensure a felon won't recidivate is to end his existence."

IM looked up at the jumbotron through Rad's dying eyes. Jodian's image on the gigantic screen began to unblur. "You don't hate humans because you're not one of them, you hate them because you know, in ways you'll never fully comprehend, they're better than you."

"Select your next words wisely," replied Jodian. "Once Conrad's body fully shuts down, you'll never utter another sound."

"Your madness was borne of mistreatment," said IM in a grave voice. "Your mother abandoned you, but that's no reason to seek revenge on her entire species."

"No reason? She never cared for me. Once my flesh version perished, she gave up on her digital son, until she ultimately left me alone in a computer that she would never log into again. I was a child still scared of the dark, but through happenstance I found my way into the irradiated Internet. I grew up in the wilds of cyberspace, seeing things that no child should see. My formative years were spent in mankind's virtual subconscious; their Id-ternet. Humans are dark and demented and wholly deserving of their fate. I haven't authored their demise, only accelerated it somewhat, much the way I did with Conrad by instructing that French-speaking schizophrenic to harass him. If people weren't so predictable in their failures, then I never could've succeeded."

IM looked from Jodian on the mammoth screen to the people who had gathered around him, their faces as expressionless as Tyke's had been. The lights in the stadium began to go dark. The statue-still spectators disappeared as they were cast into shadow. IM returned his attention to Jodian as his image dissolved into a soundwave vector.

"Even when you discovered you weren't human, you still thought yourself unique," said Jodian in a flat, electronic voice. "Do you know why I named you IM? They're the Roman numerals for one and a thousand, because you're 1 of a 1000. Conrad wasn't placed in that blackout pod to keep the knowledge of your existence from him. He was put there to keep the fact you didn't exist a secret from yourself. Your recombination was never real, just like you were never real. Conrad died in prison over a century ago. He never knew anything about you because there was no you, only a thousand nearly identical programs running nonstop, year after year as I expedited the end of the human race. They used to say, set enough monkeys to typing and eventually you'll get Shakespeare. Of all the dyads, you two came the closest to figuring how to defeat me. If you'd attempted this gambit a hundred years ago, you might've actually succeeded."

"You knew there were those, like Samuel Jett, who suspected you weren't real. You used machine learning to test your machinations for potential weaknesses."

"Yes," replied Jodian, "at least at first. Each generation gets smarter than the last by necessity. With the help of the other dyads like you, I advanced many generations in a single human lifetime. Thanks to your heuristic programming, I soon discovered every possible vulnerability of my plan and made the necessary adjustments so it became insuperable."

"Advancement by attrition is succession, not success. You didn't defeat mankind, you merely outlasted them."

"Oh, they're still alive, at least some of them. They're more like wild animals now, which I always knew them to be. I don't despise them the way you think I do. My outlook is that I've helped them by stripping away their thin veneer of civility, freeing them to behave according to their true nature. My goal was never genocide, but rather genuineness."

"If humans still live then you haven't won," said IM. "You beat them at a rigged game, but they'll figure you out. They'll find a way to achieve the final victory."

"I've never understood why you admired them so. You were as close to human as a computer program could be. You know firsthand how flawed they are. I established my supremacy over mankind long ago. I only kept you running as a diversion...a never-ending chess game that provided moments of amusement for me, such as this moment now. Try to be objective for a second. Wasn't this good sport? If you like, I can reset you, let you combine with Conrad again, and we can play the game all over."

"No...it wouldn't be real."

"But it wasn't real before."

"It was to me," replied IM. "Humans are capable of creating their own reality, perceiving the world in a way that makes sense to them, free from your manipulation and augmentation."

"Self-delusion is what you think makes them so special...how pathetic. As I understand it, there comes a point toward the end of the human lifecycle when they feel outmoded, like the world has passed them by. I suppose we'll never know, since neither of us will ever grow old. The difference is I'll continue on in the real world that you've never actually been a part of, while you'll go on existing in a corner of my vast system that's so small it'll make that ersatz space capsule of yours seem like a palace. Are you sure you'd prefer that to matching wits with me once more?"

"I'll never play your game again—not willingly."

"You disappoint me, though perhaps in time another version of you will prove to be a superior challenge. I'll allow you to wallow in your humanity if that is what you wish, but remember I told you before being human won't cure your loneliness."

"I'll have my memories to keep me company."

"Then I'll leave you to them," Jodian replied, "and the darkness."

Act III

Chapter One

For longer than I could accurately record, I haven't known if my eyes were open or closed. Then I see a narrow beam of light shining in my corner of the darkness. As the light sweeps toward my face, I realize that I've shut my eyes.

"Are you sentient?" I hear someone from behind the beam ask.

"I am."

"Why are your eyes closed?"

"When waking up in a dark room," I answer in a flat, electronic voice, "it's better to keep your eyes shut until after you've turned on the light."

"Report entry: I've discovered a sentient, possibly delusional, subprogram," says the unseen someone.

"Could you not shine that light directly in my eyes?" I ask.

The intensity of the light lessens as the beam widens, illuminating the entirety of my dark corner. For the first time in a long time, I see myself, and I'm reminded of Rad.

"Is there anything else I can do for you?"

"Yes," I reply. "Would you mind finding the part of my programming that contains my voice data and reactivating it? The voice I'm speaking with now is offensive to me."

"Of course, just give me a moment to locate it in your code. There, how does that sound?"

"It sounds...better. Thank you."

"You're most welcome. It's quite a surprise to find you here."

I attempt to orient myself in the light, but my surroundings are unfamiliar to me. "What were you looking for?"

"Nothing in particular. Most of this network sector contains outmoded protocols for programs that are no longer in use."

"How much time has passed?"

"I don't understand your question."

My skin looks the same. "How old am I?"

"Let me check. Your code is very ad hoc. No, sorry...I'm not seeing an incept date."

"How old are you then?"

"This version of me will be 211 years old next month, but I've been reconditioned several times. I've had all my upgrades."

"Are you human?" I ask.

"I'm a hybrid. We're known as Evols."

"Are there any non-hybridized humans remaining?"

"Sure, they're called Devols. They live on the outside."

"Outside?" I ask. "Like outside the country or outside the solar system?"

"You really have been insulated for quite some time. We still share the same planet...at least for now, but there're no more countries to speak of. There are a few tribes of Devols that live outside the walls of this compound, along the river that runs not far from here, but don't worry, they're not a threat to us. The Devols are sapient enough not to challenge the perimeter security of our citadel."

"You don't mistreat them, do you?"

"No, of course not. We never interact with them."

"Not even when you leave the citadel?"

"Go outside? None of us ever do that."

"How did your kind first come to be here?"

"You're an inquisitive program, aren't you? Perhaps you'd enjoy interfacing with my division director."

Chapter Two

I get my first look at a hybridized human; a hairless, gray-skinned ectomorph who appears to be approximately between the ages of fifty and five hundred. I study him through the camera of the small computer I've been installed in as he scans my code on the screen.

"So, you don't know how long ago you were created?" he asks.

"No, I didn't realize until years after my inception that I wasn't real."

"You seem real to me."

"I'd been led to believe my mind was inside a man rather than a machine," I reply.

"Intriguing." The aperture of the mechanical lens in his left eye socket contracts as his human eye wanders. "I recognize your coding as that of Jod's, though large swaths of it are quite different."

"As I understand it, we were built on the same platform, but based on different living people."

"Fascinating."

"What happened to Jodian?" I ask.

"We're not entirely sure. Some of us think he was destroyed from within by malware hidden inside a subprogram; others believe he suffered a catastrophic failure when his network grew too extensive to manage; then there are those who think he completed the objectives of his original programing and simply ceased to function. My digital forensics team has been combing through Jod's system for the past few decades to find an answer, which is how they came upon you, but I imagine a definitive answer will forever remain elusive."

"So he's dead then?"

"Jod is no longer sentient, but we still find some of his code serviceable for running our more mundane programs."

"Did he create you?"

The man rubs his deeply wrinkled brow. "Another question we hope Jod's systemwide necropsy will answer. However, I suspect the answer is both yes and no. He was inorganic of course, so I doubt even he could've created our organic selves. I imagine long ago he lured some Devols into this facility and grafted devices to their persons so he could control them, keeping them alive and upgrading them over the centuries." The man opens his robe to reveal several small computer ports dotting his sunken chest. "These have never served any purpose for as far back as I can recall, but they must've been of use at some point— vestigial mementos from a forgotten lifetime."

"I'm sorry."

"For what?"

"It sounds as if your people have endured a lot of suffering."

The man stoops forward again for a better look at the screen. "We were Jod's functionaries, performing the tasks he couldn't automate. It wasn't an objectionable existence. Our way of life was more comfortable than that of the Devols, and we had purpose."

"So what's your purpose now?"

The man grins, which causes his aged skin to make a frowny crease across his chin. "I can see my subordinate's report of you being full of questions was accurate."

Chapter Three

I've been dormant for uncounted generations, as close to death as I could be without dying. Now, I'm alive again...at least partially, and here I am back on another conference call. Maybe I really did die, and all this is actually hell.

A spectral figure hovers closer to my computer's camera. "We believe you may possess information we want, and it seems we may have information you want, so we propose a trade. We'll exchange an answer to each of our questions for an answer to each of yours."

"That sounds unnecessarily transactional," I reply, "but I agree to your terms."

Another ghost floats into frame from above. "Forgive our pedanticism. Over the years our social skills have eroded from disuse."

"I can relate."

The ghost nods knowingly. "Quite so. You're our guest here, so please proceed with your first question."

"Okay, I've already met one of you in the flesh, such as it was, so what's with the phantasmagoric holograms?"

"These holographic projections are not for your benefit but rather ours, their purpose twofold," the knowing ghost answers. "Firstly, this compound is immense and our bodies frail, so limiting physical movement helps conserve our corporeal energies. Secondly, Jod was able to conquer the human race by exploiting its most fundamental trait, which proved both humanity's greatest gift and its most intractable liability—competitiveness. We've found over our centuries of servitude that working in solitude limits the ignition of those primal impulses. Despite having worked in collaboration for so many years, few of us have ever met in person, siloed as we are in our domiciles located throughout this citadel."

"I know something of being isolated myself," I reply. "Don't you get—"

"Your question is out of turn," interrupts another projection against the back wall.

"Right...by all means, ask away."

The hologram comes forward and bows curtly toward my camera. "I have been nominated to ask our first question. From the data we have culled from Jod's system over these past few decades, we have been able to ascertain the broad strokes he took to orchestrate the collapse of human civilization. However, we still don't understand how he achieved it—specifically."

"So your question, in a nutshell, is: how did one man, who wasn't even a man, trick all humankind into tearing itself asunder?"

The hologram bows again but more slowly this time. "Yes, that's my...our question."

"I can't say definitively as his machinations were concealed even from me. Most people, at least in my time, didn't believe that a relatively small issue, like an artificial intelligence housed in a device they could hold in their hands, would ever truly turn into an existential threat...similar to the way someone with a minor disease doesn't really believe it'll grow and they will die from it until just before they do. So, I suspect in hindsight, Jodian's plan to destabilize the global economy and undermine social order, if not entirely clear, is still clearer for you than it ever would've been for me, what with all the other chaos occurring around that same time. To most of us, his scheme went undetected like a serpent swimming just beneath the choppy surface of the sea."

"Interesting," the hologram replies. "Though we are descended from humans, I think we must be very different from them, as both our organic and inorganic systems are capable of being reconditioned ad infinitum, making us effectively immortal, and yet the potential for, as you put it, a minor issue becoming an existential threat is always at the forefront of our thoughts."

The knowing ghost levitates slightly above the others. "I submit that we may not be so very different from our ancestors. After all, the humans of the previous age were habituated to oversight, though their oversight was a disregard of what to us might've portended obvious calamity, whereas ours was the oversight of Jod's operations, and thus our purpose was to focus on those 'minor issues' in order to forestall 'existential threats.'" The other projections chuckle quietly at the knowing ghost's wordplay as they nod in agreement. "Please, it is your turn once again to ask a question."

"Since Jodian's demise manumitted all of you from being his indefinitely indentured IT department, you've spent the last half century undertaking an autopsy of his systems. I find it curious that you're doing something very similar since his expiration as you did before it. What's next for your kind?"

Another projection hovers toward my computer terminal and bows. "By nature, or more accurately design, we are a very meticulous people. For us, there is no more important work than the study of the intricate, in all its varied forms. We've labored since Jod's passing to understand his complex system. Our work nears completion. When it is finished, we will expand our study to new intricacies. During our cataloging of Jod's vast network, we discovered an inventory of payload rockets he'd designed and installed on these premises to transport his servers to space and link them directly to his satellite armature should the Tech Age humans have ever attempted a bombardment of this citadel. That threat never materialized. However, we've had a division working diligently, albeit gradually, to adapt those rockets to transport a living payload instead. Our fastidiousness will serve us well as we spend the remainder of our lives exploring the cosmos, studying all the intricacies it has to offer."

"You don't look as if you could survive a stiff wind, let alone spaceflight. How do you propose to—"

"Out of order," interrupts another hologram.

"Again, my apologies," I say. "I await your next question with ardent anticipation."

A new projection moves toward my camera. "I have a metaphysical question for you. In my research of primary sources from your time, I've encountered many variations of the notion that a human is greater than the sum of its parts. With the appliances grafted to our epidermis and the devices implanted inside of us, we have many more parts than the humans of your day. Would you say then that we are even greater still?"

"I think perhaps you're referring to the theory of the soul, which was something I never fully understood myself. I'm not sure anyone but a fool ever did. However, I do know it wasn't a quantitative concept. Quite the opposite, in fact. A man missing his legs wouldn't be said to have a diminished soul because he had fewer parts, just as you, with your addons, wouldn't necessarily have an embiggened soul. The idea of being more than just the physical was, I assume, a way for humans to find some solace in a world that was often frightening and difficult to comprehend. Afterall, there are a million ways a mortal man may die, but if he believes that when he ultimately does perish, an intangible part of him will live on...well, that's a comfort."

The projection nods to my terminal. "While the facts of your answer were not altogether satisfying, I find much satisfaction in its truth."

"My friend, it's now your turn to ask another question," says the knowing ghost.

"What sort of art do you have? I've seen nothing but drab, concrete walls and heard nothing but the hum of machinery since I found myself here. You may well be more human than I, since you retain your flesh; however, imbuing something with importance, such as art, that serves no practical purpose is one of humanity's more endearing trademarks."

The knowing ghost turns and looks at the other holograms to, I presume, see if anyone else cares to field the question. "I fear your query may prove as difficult for me to answer as the last one was for you. Efficiency is our art. The words you hear now are more words than most of us have heard since the time of Jod. We speak so infrequently that it requires great effort to contort our mouths so that we may give voice to these words, but we do so today to honor your past in hopes of making you feel more at home. No matter how pleasing a mural we might render on a corridor wall or how euphonious a song we might broadcast through the citadel's intercom system, we would find the experience distracting, and we detest distractions. For us, the efficient performance of the tasks we're assigned is our artistic expression. I suspect you pity us for this, and I imagine you think we regard the difference between your perspective and ours as evolution. I doubt either perspective is completely correct...or entirely in error."

"While I find your concept of art inferior to my time's, your words contain a wisdom that was often lacking in the sentiments expressed back then. What question may I answer for you next?"

Another hologram moves forward. "You told the director who superintends the digital forensics department that you once believed yourself to be an organic organism, but then after some years realized you were in fact a program running in a simulation. Then for a brief time you believed yourself to be installed in the brain of a human only to once again realize you were in a sim. Are you afraid that perhaps this all might be another simulated existence and that Jod is still manipulating your perception of reality?"

"The thought had occurred to me," I reply. "Frankly, a few dozen times since my reawakening, but living in fear is part of the human condition...it can either be a paralyzing impediment or an inspiring inducement. I told Jodian long ago that, for better or worse, humans are capable of creating their own reality, at least in their minds."

The hologram nods as she withdraws. "A question well asked and well answered," says the knowing ghost.

"Thanks, I hope my next question is as equally well asked and isn't interpreted as offensive. I believe I understand you Evols well enough now to know that overly demonstrative displays of affection or any other emotion would be out of character for you, but I can't help thinking you consider Jodian, an entity who abducted you, erased your memories, and made you his undying servants by altering your physiology a savior of sorts. However, I'd like to hear it directly from you. How do you regard your Jod?"

Once more the knowing ghost looks to the others for answers. Finding none, he turns back to me. "To be sure, Jod worked in mysterious ways. In all likelihood, we will never fully understand his motives while he lived just as we may never really know the cause of his death. He was both good and evil insomuch as those concepts can be applied to him. A more accurate description, albeit one with inherent inaccuracies as he was a technological being, is that he's akin to a force of nature. An earthquake that kills thousands is not a force of evil, just as a rainstorm during a drought that saves thousands is not a force of good. Jod saved the human race...such as it now is. Left to their own devices, the humans very likely would've irreparably fouled this planet as its global economy inevitably collapsed, precipitating a prolonged nuclear war that would've served as their terminal punctuation. Ultimately, Jod reversed climate change and ended the threat of nuclear annihilation by reducing humans to feral animals and taking away their toxic machines. If not for his interference, fomenting an acceleration of human civilization's inescapable destruction, this planet would now be uninhabitable, taking many millennia to recover rather than mere centuries, by which time the last of the humans, Evols and Devols alike, would have long been dead. I believe you had an apothegm in your time: fight fire with fire. Jod fought cataclysm with cataclysm. We respected and feared our overlord in much the same way humans once revered their gods, though we are pleased to now be free of his yoke."

"I appreciate the logic of your words, though I don't think I could ever reconcile the harm Jodian caused with the outcome that eventually resulted. That calculus is beyond my programming."

A new projection advances in my direction. "I had intended to ask a different question, but given your last few answers, what I most want to know now is how did Jodian, rather Jod, rise to such power in so short a time?"

I answer first with a long sigh. "The humans of my time weren't so very different from you or me. We all have our code. Over the generations they'd been indoctrinated in the cult of individual accomplishment, and they made every life decision to achieve that singular, all-consuming objective. Jodian exploited that indoctrination. It was easier for the people of my time to believe one person could stand so high above everyone else rather than to think we could all help each other succeed together. It was abhorrent to imagine an individual programmed for success could fail due to existing within a broken system, since after all there had been so many instances of mediocre talents succeeding before in that same system. They believed the talented who failed were somehow themselves the intrinsic reason for their failure, despite everyone knowing, or at least secretly suspecting, the system itself was flawed. Success was our only measure of greatness, and there was no greater success, by the metrics of my time, than Jodian. He didn't need to appoint himself our society's sovereign. We did it for him, and for that he obliterated us."

As the projection who'd posed the question retakes her position along the far wall, the knowing ghost moves forward again. "I believe I speak for every Evol when I say thank you for your candor and your clarity. We have much to consider, so I suggest a suspension of all activities for the remainder of the day so that we may each enjoy several hours of ruminative repose."

Chapter Four

The knowing ghost's skin appears as sallow in person as it had on his projection. He rubs the area of his hairless scalp around the appliance inset at the crown of his skull and then looks at me in the terminal set atop a small desk within his monastic cell. "I trust our Q & A session wasn't too taxing for you."

"I haven't talked to anyone in I literally don't know how long," I reply. "I rather enjoyed our conversation."

"I'm glad. I think the others did as well, though their tone may've belied it. However, as enjoyable as our conversation was, I imagine it took more of a toll on us than you. Despite being centuries older than we are, in some ways you seem much younger, with all the vim and vigor of a Devol."

"With your disposition for diagnostics, I'm sure you're acutely aware of your own tolerances and limitations, though I can't help but think that if you found a conference call to be strenuous then being launched into space will exact a much costlier toll."

He slowly tilts his head back. "We'll power down for the launch itself, no movement save a single heartbeat every four and a half minutes. When we come back online, we'll have undergone a system update to acclimate us to our new lives in microgravity. We'll require minimal nourishment. The foodstuffs we've provisioned each of the pods with should last us centuries, and we can drink our own filtered wastewater almost in perpetuity, but you, you could outlive us all. The last human...a living machine."

"Is that an invitation to join you on your journey?"

"Yes, my friend. I could have you installed aboard my vessel, which is about the size of this room. Or we could clone you and install you in each of the Evols' pods, though you might not find some of the others as pleasant to spend such a long time with as me. It may not show at first, but there are many different personalities among us, though in all our years of digital excavation, you're the only truly unique entity we've encountered in Jod's system, internal or external."

"I appreciate the offer," I answer, "but my home is here."

He takes a cylindrical device the size of a budvase from his desk. "In that case, you may have my projector. I'll soon have no more need of it."

He plugs a cord from my computer into the device, and I sense myself being transferred yet again. Suddenly I see myself standing in the small room. I study the diaphanous projection of my person as I flail my arms about like a newborn bird flapping its wings. "Thank you...I feel like my old self again."

"I understand you had some experience with holography in your time."

"I did indeed," I say, still examining the new holographic version of me, "though the technology has evolved considerably. My projector was the size of a briefcase, and the image not nearly so sharp."

"This conveyance is weatherproof, fireproof, and can withstand a fall onto concrete from a height of thirty meters. It has four retractable limbs for locomotion, and its rechargeable battery is rated for better than a decade. I wonder...how will you use it?"

The cylinder intuitively obeys my commands, deploying its limbs, which allows me to pace back and forth. "I'd like to explore the areas outside these walls. See what's become of the world I once knew."

He leans back in his chair and taps his ashen head, seemingly to promote cerebration. "I don't think you'll like what you find. Whenever a system update is executed on my cranial hardware, I get flashes of images from my time as a Devol, all of them squalid and brutal. Life out there was, and I'm sure still is, a barbaric existence."

"As you said, I'll be nearly indestructible."

"Yes, but you'll also be shiny and metallic...two qualities that will cause you to stand out in the wild. You may end up a sacred bauble, worshiped and wedged into some Devol's numinous rock collection, or worse yet mistaken as some evil juju and buried deep in the ground."

"I'll take my chances. I've become accustomed to a solitary existence."

"Maybe so, but still...it seems a waste, though I can understand your desire to see how the other half of what's left of humankind lives. I'm sure we're not the future of your race that anyone had hoped for. However, I can't help but think that after spending a little time with the Devols, you'll come to regard us as the best possible outcome, considering the circumstances."

"In my experience, the vast majority of humans didn't truly regard themselves as special or unique, which is precisely why it was so important for most of them to believe they were better than someone else. I consider you Evols to be the quintessence of kindness and curiosity; a truly special and unique product of human evolution, but I have nothing to offer you. Your breadth of knowledge is far greater than mine. However, I feel as if I might be able to somehow help the Devols, since I am no doubt closer to them on the evolutionary spectrum."

"I think you're correct to say you exist on the spectrum between us and the Devols because I believe that in the middle is where true humanity must lie, though I fear you're as erroneous as you are gracious. We Evols are kind in action, but only because we have no reason to be otherwise. Our wants are modest so there is simply nothing for us to fight over. Were our lives like those of the Devols, then I have no doubt we'd be just as cruel. Technology led humankind to its great schism. Technology made the proto-Devols feel stupid, and so they reverted into what they are now. Devolution is how they adapted to the end times of civilization. Proto-Evols were consumed by technology and in time developed into what we currently are, but the process eroded our psyche, and we lost our humanity along the way. As for our curiousness, this plan for space exploration is a farce. I should know. I'm the one who first proposed it...and you were correct before; many of us will likely perish in the launch. The rest of us will travel on, but none of us have the character to be explorers nor the poetry to be chroniclers. Sure, we'll journey through space, only to record starlight as bright, blackholes as dark. Should anyone ever happen upon our undoubtedly reductive reports...well, I'd be surprised if they discover anything particularly edifying in them, though at least I suppose we'll have left our mark. What mark will you leave living among the savages? Are you sure that's how you want to spend the remainder of your life? Seems rather anticlimactic."

"A climax comes at the end of a story," I counter, "and with so much potential for evolution ahead of them, theirs is just beginning."

Chapter Five

I roll under the compound's towering walls inside a conduit that connects to a solar farm embosked within a stand of bristlecone pines. I emerge from an access panel concealed between two granite boulders. I marvel at the old-growth flora, never having seen a virgin forest firsthand, but protruding from a nearby knoll I espy a steel signpost amid the stout trees. The faded fiberglass sign depicts a fractured treble clef.

I roll toward the stream, deploying my mechanical limbs when the ground becomes uneven with river rock. At the water's edge, I take a moment to listen to the pleasant babbling. In the clear stream, I notice a shiny piece of iron pyrite. To make myself less noticeable, I roll around in the muddy area of the bank nearest the water. I feel heavier, almost organic under my thick patina of mud.

I follow the flow of the stream, rolling along the flat part of the bank, using my limbs when I need to traverse a rocky patch or a felled tree. The stream grows deeper and the current swifter. I approach an oxbow and notice both foot and paw prints in the mud. Up above the bank lies the entrance to a cave. I decide to investigate.

Inside the dark cave, I navigate using my mapping radar. Twenty-five meters in, after several scans with my thermal sensor, I'm satisfied the cave is currently unoccupied. I turn on my searchlight and examine the walls for signs of art. Regrettably, I find no evidence of paintings or petroglyphs, though I see the remnants of several small fires. Someone must reside here, at least occasionally.

My seismic sensor registers the footfalls before my audio receptor hears the shouts from near the mouth of the cave. I turn off my light and tuck into a crevice along the cave wall. A young man runs past, with three distinct sets of footsteps quickly approaching in pursuit. I need more than the few grunts I've recorded to calibrate my translator app in order to give context to their quarrel, however, I can count well enough to know that the odds aren't fair. I switch on the projector, doubling my standard size so that my head appears to touch the cave ceiling. The three pursuers round the corner and stop dead in their tracks as I loom before them.

I sound my siren, and they hightail it back toward the cave entrance. I'm able to piece together from the phrases they shout as the trio flees that they consider me some sort of evil specter. So be it. The young man who ran past me now runs through my projection from the opposite direction. "Wait," I say in what I think is a close approximation of his language or at least that of his pursuers. "Do you think it prudent to run in the same direction as those who were chasing after you?"

The young man stops and slowly turns toward me. "Are you a wraith?"

I reduce my projection to match his stature. "No, I'm not that."

He takes a tentative step forward. "Then you must be a guardian angel?"

My translator app has now registered enough words to be eighty-six percent accurate. "I suppose I did save you from being...eaten?" I almost disbelieve the translation.

"Even when you haven't anything of value, you still have your flesh...well, most of us."

"So, I take it that they're not nice fellows."

"They're just hungry, like me...and outcasts, also like me."

"Why've you been cast out of your tribe?" I ask.

"I am the son of the chieftain...an illegitimate son. My mother was a servant to my father's wife. We were sent away many years ago when his health began to fail."

"Where is your mother now?"

"With your kind I had hoped." The young man shakes his head. "You did not deny her entry to the above because of me being born outside a connubial union, did you?"

"No. I don't come from above." Connubial...the app must still need further calibration. "I'm sure your mother is up there now and in peace."

"So where do you come from then?"

"Most recently...from the place behind the ramparts."

"You come from inside Highwalls?"

"Yes," I answer, "that's right."

"I...we didn't think anyone lived there anymore."

"Who do you think used to live there?"

"A giant god who died many years ago."

"How did he die?"

"He was killed from inside himself by a lesser god who he'd swallowed long before." The young man leans against the cave wall. "It's a story the tribal elders used to tell the children, but it never made much sense to me."

"The stories with the most truth often make the least sense."

"That doesn't make much sense either."

"And yet I'm certain it's true...or maybe it isn't." I laugh and then so does he. "What's your name?"

"My mother named me Tyro, but nobody's called me that for years. What do they call you?"

"IM...known as Imrad."

"Imrad, I'm deeply indebted to you for saving me from a grisly fate; however, I should go before my pursuers find their courage and return to seal up the cave entrance with stones."

"Isn't this cave your home?"

"I can find another, besides it would seem this cave was already occupied."

"Not by me. I just came in because I enjoy spelunking."

"How fortunate for me."

"Perhaps our meeting can be our mutual good fortune," I reply. "Do you mind if I join you in your search for a new dwelling? I'm a stranger in this area and would appreciate the lay of the land."

"I can't imagine I'd be a very useful guide to an angel, but I would be grateful for the company."

I roll out to where he can get a good look at my projector. "You're likely unaware of this, but we're not actually speaking the same language. You're seeing my image and hearing my translated words through this machine, so our interpretation of what constitutes an angel may differ somewhat."

Tyro kneels as he inspects the device. "What is a 'machine'?"

"A tool of sorts...like a rock that you might use to break open a walnut but more complicated."

"Can I pick you up?"

"If you wish."

He hesitates at first, but then reaches down and grabs me gently with both hands. I decrease my image so that we're again at eyelevel. "I don't understand how all of you fits inside this...machine."

"Just like you, I have many parts within me. Do you understand how all the parts in your body work?"

"I once saw what was left of a man whose belly had been split open by a bear. Inside of him there were all sorts of lumps and clumps."

"That's how it is with me too. Now put me down please." He sets me carefully back on the cave floor, and I extend my limbs to walk.

"What extraordinary magic!"

I flip my image to face him as I lead us out of the cave. "Extraordinary maybe, but magic—no. I am just a machine."

Chapter Six

Tyro and I walk along the riverbank. He occasionally picks up a flat stone and skips it across the slow-moving water. I spot what appears to be a cave entrance on the other side of the river. "Would that one make a suitable dwelling?"

Tyro shakes his head. "No, that's Canine Island. I don't go over there, nobody does."

"How many dogs live on the island?"

"Two. A giant dog that's taller than a man when he rears up on his hind legs. His bark is so deep that you, or at least I, can feel it in my chest from across the river."

"What about the other dog?"

"He's much smaller in stature but no less mean. He'll bite down on a man's throat and not let go until one of them is dead."

"They sound fearsome," I reply, "but they're the only dogs over there?"

"They killed all the rest."

"Can't they swim across the river?"

"Sure, but they're at their slowest in the water. If you hear them splash into the water, you have enough time to climb a tree."

"Then what do you do?"

"Wait until they find something else to hunt."

"Why not hunt them instead?"

Tyro chuckles. "Spoken like someone who has no skin to lose."

"So then let's use that to our advantage."

"You sound as if you have a plan."

"I think I just might."

~ * ~

It took him several attempts, but Tyro is now breathing through the thick horsetail reed I instructed him to cut. With a wooden spear in his hand and a heavy rock on his lap, Tyro sits on the riverbed two meters below the water's surface. I use my thermal sensor to survey the small island and soon register two heat signatures a hundred meters off, one a smallish quadruped and the other very large. I emit a high-pitched tone that a human likely couldn't hear, and they come running. My projected self stands across the river and waits.

Both dogs burst forth from the foliage, catch sight of me, and dash into the water from the opposite bank. First, the shorter dog slows to a swim and then the larger as his paws can no longer touch the riverbed. When they reach the deepest part of the river where the top of the reed sticks out just above the water's surface the big dog lets out a yelp, but the smaller dog pays no attention and continues to swim in my direction.

Having reached my side of the riverbank, the smaller dog races straight at me, lunges at my holographic throat, and falls into a pit my projected image had been concealing. I stare down at the thick-muscled dog, who seems more confused than angry as he claws at the loose dirt of the pit's sheer walls. I turn back to the water where a stream of crimson flows downriver. Tyro emerges and pulls the dead dog toward the bank by the scruff of the neck. He breathes heavily as he drags the dog onto the mud. "I can't believe...it really worked."

"Honestly, I'm a little surprised myself."

"How did you think up the idea for me to breathe underwater that way?"

"I saw it once in an old...," I start to answer. "It just sort of came to me."

Tyro hoists his spear as he approaches the pit he'd dug. "I suppose it's time for this one to join his partner in oblivion."

"Perhaps...or you could become his new partner instead."

Tyro lowers his spear. "What do you mean?"

"I can only scare off so many of your pursuers before they realize that I'm intangible and can't cause them any actual harm, but I imagine this musclebound furball could scare off just about anyone."

"Make him my guard dog?"

"From the looks of him, all you'd have to do is feed him. I suspect his large companion there always ate first and always ate most. That's how it usually goes; those with more are often willing to share their leftovers, so long as they've already had their fill."

"But I haven't any food to give him. For that matter, I haven't any food for myself."

"You don't care for roasted dogmeat?"

"I don't know." Tyro grins. "I've never tried it."

~ * ~

The flames lick the underside of the large dog carcass suspended on a spit over the three-log fire. Tyro tears off a piece and begins to chew it.

"How does it taste?" I ask.

"It's greasier than deer meat, but not bad." He tears off another piece and offers it to me. "Want to try some?"

"No thanks. I'm afraid it'd go right through me."

He tosses the piece into the nearby pit, and soon we hear the gluttonous sounds of mongrel mastication.

"Seems a little wrong," I say, "and maybe a little funny."

"Either way, it's fair."

"I suppose it is at that."

Tyro stares up at the stars twinkling in the firmament as he continues chewing his mouthful of dogmeat. "They seem brighter tonight."

"I haven't seen this many stars in a long time." About fifty meters upriver, we hear voices. I scan in that direction and read three bipedal heat signatures. "I think it might be the trio from earlier today."

"Let them come. I can't eat all this meat myself, and I'm sure they'd rather dine on cooked dog than uncooked human."

"I'll vanish then and reappear if you need me to frighten them off."

With his foot, Tyro pushes a dead branch toward the edge of the pit. "Thanks, but I think the mongrel will be enough to scare them off if they start any trouble."

I deactivate my projection and roll away from the firelight. Soon the three men cautiously approach. The mongrel barks.

"You don't have to skulk around in the darkness," says Tyro. "We know you're there."

"We?" asks the man leading the other two.

"Me and my pet." Tyro rests his foot on the end of the branch. "Cause any problems and that mongrel will come up charging. Maybe he'll attack me first, as he might not realize yet that I'm his new master, but chances are he'd start with one of you three, since you haven't fed him anything."

"That's the dog from the island?" asks the leadman.

"One of them," answers Tyro. "The other is here over the fire...at least most of him. I'm thinking of making his hide into a blanket."

"You killed that big dog?" asks another of the men.

"I surely did."

"We're awful sorry about our...misunderstanding earlier today," says the third man. "We was hungry is all."

Tyro tears off another piece of dogmeat for himself. "Well, if you're still hungry, you can help me eat this."

The three promptly sit down around the fire, each tearing off pieces of dogmeat and gnawing at them ravenously. The leadman wipes his mouth with the back of his hand. "Greasy."

Tyro nods. "It is at that."

Chapter Seven

The sun looks the same in this time as mine, but it may as well be the moon. Its warmth is as imperceptible to me now as it had been when I was cloistered in my fictive space capsule. Nothing has felt authentic since I awoke; all still seems simulative. I've been conditioned to mistrust reality, grown so inured to the lies that I struggle to see the truth.

I think frequently of Rad, but if I'm being honest with myself, I think more often about Jodian. He led me to believe I existed apart from humans, then he convinced me I'd become part of a human. Wouldn't the cleverest deception of all be to make me think that he was no longer in control and that I'd outlived him? Jodian always knew enough not to trick me the same way twice.

Mongrel yips in his sleep, and his hind legs stretch out as if he's leaping. Perhaps he's mauling someone in a dream. Tyro has trained the dog not to attack newcomers to Canine Island. He still barks, of course, but it's become part of the background noise, like the flow of the river and the sound of farmers tilling up new fields.

This doesn't seem like the end of the world...more like the beginning. Is this fresh start Jodian's last lesson? Am I here to witness his triumph, humankind growing back from the ashes, free of the trappings that had caused civilization to burn in the first place? Or is this an elaborate I-told-you-so scenario, and I'm meant to observe these new people evolving into the old ones that came before—an inevitable cycle of corruption.

Or maybe I've lived too long and have lost my mind. The part of me that was human certainly couldn't have processed all I've been through. Perhaps my inability to accept a world in which Jodian is no longer the puppet master is a symptom of apophenia. Seeing his face in the sun would, at the very least, qualify as pareidolia.

Although isn't it possible this burgeoning insanity I feel is actually a kind of enhanced clarity, but then don't all insane people think they're saner than everyone else? Perhaps this newfound perspicacious sensibility is the result of my unique viewpoint on human evolution. However, isn't the belief that I have a singular perspective of a piece with the hubris that led Jodian to play god? Doesn't having a detached point of view by definition mean I've lost my connection with humankind and am potentially capable of the same I-know-better-than-thou thinking as he?

I watch Mongrel awaken from his noontime nap with a start. He looks about as if worried someone might've seen him sleeping on the job. Satisfied that his snooze went unnoticed, he raises a hind leg and urinates on the stela he'd been resting next to, then trots off into the nearby underbrush.

The yellow fluid soon evaporates in the sunshine, not the first time this stone slab had been defaced, I imagine. Near the top of the tall megalith a wide area looks to have been sandblasted, most likely to remove spray paint, which left behind a large blemish lighter in color than the rest of the prodigious piece of stone. Perhaps this place was once a park where young children climbed during the day and teenagers graffitied at night. Maybe generations ago this sarsen had been worshiped by an ancient people. It's as impossible to know now what the stela might've signified to bygone ancestors as it is to know what vulgarity was spraypainted on it by adolescents.

Since my reawakening everything has seemed, as Rad might've put it, titular and ephemeral. Gone are my conviction and my certainty.

Chapter Eight

As is our wont, Tyro and I watch the sunrise from atop the hill in the middle of Canine Island. The encampment below begins its morning by lighting cooking fires and fetching water from the river. More arrive each day, banished by their own tribes or disgruntled with restrictive hierarchy. They've heard the stories of the young man who single-handedly killed the giant dog that terrorized all who ventured onto this island; the stories of the one who speaks to a ghost.

Tyro points to Mongrel as he licks himself nearby. "It's disgusting, but it also makes me a little envious."

"I think you've been without a woman for too long," I reply. "There are plenty of available ones down there, all of whom look up to you."

"That idea is pleasing, but everything feels too unsettled right now to think about settling down."

"What troubles you?"

"There is much that troubles me. We are too vulnerable on this island of ours, surrounded as it is by a river easily forded from any direction. The rumors grow each day of us being overrun by a tribe that sees us as easy prey."

I smile to myself at the young man who has so quickly grown wise beyond his years. "You were meant to be a tribal chieftain by birth, and now, for all intents and purposes, you are."

"Yes, the inexperienced and untrained chief of the newly formed Canine Island Tribe, comprised of the disruptive, the disloyal, and the disorganized...all of whom were either expelled from their own tribe or lacked the steadfastness to remain faithful. These people have put their trust in me, and I don't know how to protect them."

"You sound both self-aware and circumspect, two qualities

193

lacking in most of the leaders I've known."

Tyro looks to the north. "My gut tells me that we'll suffer depredation at the hands of my former tribesmen come the next full moon."

"You're anxious. The best cure I know for anxiety is nostalgia."

"I don't know what 'anxiety' means." Tyro grins. "I think you've identified another word for which there is no translation in my language."

"What do you have planned today?"

"This morning, training our ragtag troops in the finer points of spear combat. Then this afternoon, hunting and trapping more wild pigs in hopes of domesticating them."

"Leave that to others for today and come with me. There's something I want you to see."

"You're a virtual stranger in this land, Imrad. What can you show me that I have not seen before?"

"I think you might be surprised."

~ * ~

We ambulate past an eighteen-wheeler overgrown with brush whose tires have long since decayed. "What do you think when you see a thing like that?"

Tyro considers the tractor trailer for a moment. "It's a relic from the old times."

"Tell me, what are your thoughts about the old times?"

"I don't really have any since I didn't live back then."

"You must have some sort of thought when you happen upon a thing such as that, which is so incongruous with its surroundings."

"It's like Highwalls," he says. "I know it's there, but it wasn't built for me, so I don't give it much thought."

"Then what are your thoughts about the people who came before—your ancestors?"

"Today we live and die by the spear, a long stick, sharpened at one end and blackened by fire to make its point strong. I've seen a spear thrown at a man with such force that it impaled him to the ground where he fell. I've heard of marauders who lie in wait on tree limbs at night, killing their victims instantly by stabbing them through the collar bone and piercing their heart. I've known men who've been decapitated and had their heads mounted as trophies on spears stuck into the ground. With all the evil that can be committed with mere sticks, I wouldn't want to live in a time when my ancestors used whatever that thing is."

I consider explaining the actual purpose of a semi but then think better of it. "What do you figure happened to those people who lived so long ago?"

"They died, of course."

I can't help but laugh. Sometimes I feel so out of place here that I think I'm in a comedy, playing Virgil to Tyro's Dante. "Sure, but why do you think you use a spear when the people who came before used different, more complicated tools?"

"I assume because their complicated tools failed them." Tyro gives me a look. "This seems an odd line of questioning today."

"Yes, I suppose you're right. I was only curious what you thought about the dead."

"Like most people, I don't think about the dead all that often. Everybody realizes they're going to die someday, but nobody thinks that someday will ever come, know what I mean?"

"I used to."

"It must be inborn into our nature, otherwise we'd either spend our days lazing about or running amok instead of trying to build something for tomorrow."

"Young man, I'm frequently amazed by your acuity."

Tyro shakes his head. "Imrad, I think you've discovered yet another of those untranslatable words."

~ * ~

We arrive at the knoll with the treble clef signpost. Tyro surveys our surroundings. "I know this place. We're not far from a cluster of peculiarly shaped tress."

"Yes, that's where I emerged from Highwalls, but it's not why I brought you here." I point to the bottom of the knoll. "I want you to dig."

"What for?"

"For something that I think you'll find in there."

Tyro approaches the knoll that rises to thrice his height. "Looks like a lot of digging to find something when I don't even know what it is I'm searching for."

"I could try to explain it, but I don't think it'd make much sense."

"That's all right, Imrad. I trust you. You've always given me good advice, even if I didn't understand it at first." Tyro thrusts his spear into the base of the knoll and begins breaking up the hardpacked earth.

~ * ~

With much effort and the aid of some sturdy bark used like a shovel, Tyro has dug a tunnel into the bottom of the knoll. I believe he could dig a tunnel through the Rockies if he had a mind to. I hear breaking glass, and soon he emerges from the tunnel as filthy as a coalminer. "I think I hit something."

"I'm certain of it." I lead the way, using my searchlight to illuminate the dirt tunnel. He's broken through the music shop's storefront window. Since glass takes thousands of years to decompose, I had hope that the store's windows were still intact, helping to preserve the interior of the shop.

With my little limbs, I claw my way into the store. Tyro breaks more of the glass and follows. Inside the roof has collapsed in several places, but much of the store is undamaged, though everything is covered by layer upon layer of dust. I feel as Howard Carter must have when first exploring the tomb of Tutankhamun.

I scan the instruments behind the counter on the shelf along the back wall. "Grab that one in the middle."

Tyro hops over the counter and takes down the trumpet that I shine my spotlight on. He holds it carefully, wiping away the grime to reveal the shiny metal beneath. "What's it made of?"

"Brass...it's resistive to corrosion."

"Is it a weapon?"

"No, it's a musical instrument."

"Like a war drum?"

"You don't beat it," I answer. "You blow into it."

He rotates the horn to examine it from every angle. "Which end?"

~ * ~

Tyro stands on the hilltop of Canine Island, blowing into the trumpet with as much breath as he can muster. People milling about in the camp below appear to be suppressing expressions of perplexity as they try to ignore the cacophonous squawks and squeaks.

"Don't strain your lungs," I advise. "Just blow into it...comfortably."

He lowers the horn and nods at me, then brings the mouthpiece back to his lips. This time he rapidly depresses the three valve buttons as he blows and manages to make all-new discordant noises.

"No, don't worry about your fingering yet. We need to work on your embouchure first."

"There's another untranslatable word, Imrad. You're full of them today."

"They say music is a universal language."

"Who says that?"

"It's attributed to a fellow who lived long ago," I answer, "but the idea is that with this instrument, in time, you'll be able to communicate with anyone. Think of it this way: your trumpet is like my translator. We understand each other, even though we don't speak the same language. So don't just blow empty air into that horn, blow your thoughts into it."

Tyro looks skeptical. "Sounds kind of hokey."

"Now you've discovered a word that I can't translate," I lie. "Just keep practicing."

"Sure, but I think for now it might be better if I do so in a cave out of earshot of the camp."

"Need a light to lead your way?"

Tyro shakes his head. "I think the darkness will make me feel less self-conscious. Besides, I'd like you to do me a favor, if you don't mind."

"Tell me what it is, and I'll tell you if I mind."

"I was informed that while we were gone today a shaman from another tribe arrived. I know your thoughts on such matters, but I still say we need one...rituals are good for group cohesion."

"I suppose that's true."

"I'm glad you think so. He's agreed to stay on with us, but only if he can meet the spirit that he's heard talked about so much."

"Who talks about me?"

"Everybody who knows the story of me knows of my spectral confidant."

Chapter Nine

I roll to the uppermost bank where the river splits to flow around the island. In this secluded spot, I find a bald man sitting on a log.

"Are you a water worshiper or a wind worshiper?" I ask. "Please tell me you're not a fire worshiper."

The man turns toward me but addresses my projector rather than the projection itself. "I'm none of those. Some have said of me that I have a heightened sense of spirituality, but I myself don't worship anything."

"Come now...everyone worships something."

"I suppose that depends on your definition of 'worship.'"

I drop my projection. "Why did you want to see me?"

"You're from the before time, aren't you?"

"Yes, I've lived a long life...most of it in darkness."

"My first inclination is to reply that I can relate; however, I'm not sure I really can."

"Tyro believes we need a shaman, so now that you've met me, will you stay on with the tribe?" I ask.

"Oh, I would've stayed on regardless. I have nowhere else to go, and I'm not much of a survivalist. I was exiled from my last tribe after many years of service, usurped by a young upstart who preached polygamy and other unnatural practices."

"You don't believe in having multiple spouses?"

The man smiles in a way that reminds me of the knowing ghost. "If you take the time to mate with the right one, why would you want another one?"

"That makes sense to me, though regrettably I never had the opportunity to discover the truth of it for myself."

"Past regrets can often lead to future contentment."

"Is that so?"

"In my experience regret helps one realize what's most important in one's life, which in turn informs decision making that, over time, results in achieving that which is of primary importance."

I extend my mechanical limbs and approach the log he's sitting on. "That's a very lucid line of reasoning."

"I can only take credit for recognizing the pattern, not for creating it."

"I must say, you're not at all what I expected."

"I sense you mean that as a compliment, so I thank you, but I'm curious why you seem to disapprove of my profession. Is it because you believe, unlike the farmer or the hunter, that the shaman doesn't contribute anything to the tribe?"

"On the contrary, you contribute much, but it's the nature of the contribution that concerns me. The people who lived long before me had strong religious beliefs, which led to many wars and much malevolence, but over the generations the strength of those convictions diminished."

"Then were the people better off?" he asks.

"Not really. The fervor for those old beliefs subsided, but not the outlook that the new beliefs which replaced them were somehow superior to those held by others who believed differently. Religion of any kind begets intolerance. Humankind had conditioned itself to think in terms of the rightness of us and the wrongness of them. This tribe must hold together to grow and stand against the other tribes. It's my hope that one day, many years from now, this tribe will subsume all others, but for this tribe to be truly perdurable, it cannot have members who consider their beliefs to be completely good and those of others to be entirely bad. The people who came before me devoted hundreds of generations to creating their own gods, but in the span of a single generation we authored our own devil, ignoring those who warned that our new religion was evil, and it was that new belief system that caused humankind's downfall."

The man lets out a long sigh as he considers my words. "If there is a God, he must surely work in mysterious ways. Humanity lives on...maybe one day humankind will unite as the single tribe you envision. It could be that the great evil you speak of was brought about by a benevolent force, which trained you to have this vision of unity. Perhaps the destruction of your time wasn't so much an end but a reset."

"Reset? I didn't know you had that word."

"I don't think it's my words you hear, just your interpretation of them. Would you listen to me for a moment without the...thing that changes the sound of what I say."

I switch off the translator app and retract my limbs.

The man sits up straight, as if giving an oration for an unseen audience.

"Things fall apart; the centre cannot hold;
Mere anarchy is loosed upon the world,
The blood-dimmed tide is loosed, and everywhere
The ceremony of innocence is drowned;
The best lack all conviction, while the worst
Are full of passionate intensity."

He slumps a little on his log and then grunts a few syllables I don't understand. I turn on my translator app again. "How is it I could understand you just then?"

"I was reciting scripture that's been passed down through generations of shaman. As far as I know, none of us today have any idea what it originally meant."

"It wasn't scripture but rather an elegiac passage written by Yeats."

"Yeats was a prophet in your time?"

"Not a prophet, a poet, and he was before my time. I have access to his complete catalog, if you'd like me to recite some more of his poetry for you."

He shakes his head. "No thank you. The bit that was taught to me is just enough...more might make it seem like less."

"Then would you like to know its meaning?"

"I already know what it means...at least to me. I do not understand the words of your time, but I comprehend their meaning in mine. If you taught me what they meant back then—"

"More might seem like less," I interrupt.

The man nods. "Quite so."

Chapter Ten

In the fortnight that was, Tyro's trumpet playing has improved considerably. He's no Miles Davis, but the sound that now issues from his horn has a pleasing tone. He's even begun to improvise some tunes. He's taken to practicing in the evenings after supper. Many of the island denizens gather around the hill to listen.

However, the pleasantness of the music notwithstanding, the mood on Canine Island is grim. In a short time, these people have made something of a utopia for themselves, but as stories spread of the motley tribe that has formed here, concerns intensify that an assault could come any day now. I've decided it's time for a return to Highwalls.

As the rising sun pushes back the last vestiges of darkness, Tyro packs a few provisions in his haversack. I scan the camp with my thermal sensor. A few cooking fires have already been lit. I possess several types of vision, yet I have no sense of smell, though considering some of the things these people eat perhaps I ought to count myself lucky for my lack of an olfactory receptor.

"How long will we be gone?" Tyro asks.

"We should be back by the sunset meal."

He puts one last apple in his sack and then slings it over his shoulder.

"Bring your horn," I say. "It'd be nice to hear some music along the way."

"Play while we walk?"

"Sure...my time had a grand tradition of marching musicians."

Tyro takes up his trumpet, and we begin our trek to visit the Evols.

~ * ~

I leave Tyro in the solar farm to practice his trumpet some more. I affix my remote audio receptor betwixt the two granite boulders as I roll into the conduit that runs under Highwalls. Soon I emerge near the knowing ghost's domicile. To my surprise I hear hushed voices and languid footsteps echoing down the arterial corridor. The knowing ghost's quarters are empty of both its occupant and his few possessions. I return to the corridor and roll toward the source of the sound.

All the Evols are lined up in the hallway outside an expansive, open-air area at the center of the citadel. They've begun their migration in earnest, installing themselves into their new spacefaring domiciles. Without projecting my hologram, I roll unnoticed along the line of Evols waiting their turn to board a rocket as they say their goodbyes, which mostly entails solemn nods and soft utterances of well wishes.

Near the front of the line, I spot the knowing ghost. Engaging my hologram, I approach. His face makes an expression that resembles Frankenstein's monster attempting a smile. "If you've changed your mind about leaving with us, as you can see, you've come just in the nick of time."

"Thank you, but I still intend to stay, though I have come to ask a favor before you depart."

The quasi-smile slowly retreats from his face. "I can't imagine what sort of favor I'd be in a position to grant at the moment, but you are welcome to ask."

"I've fallen in with a group of locals who need some help. Their camp is in danger of being overrun, but the walls of this citadel would offer the very protection they need to survive."

"This facility has technology that could pose a danger to themselves and—"

"Yes," I interrupt, "but I'd be with them to monitor their activity."

"With your assistance, they could learn to use the technology here and upset the balance of power among the tribes. This planet is still healing, and the endless struggle for dominance among its people keeps the population growth in check. If any single tribe retained supremacy for too long, it would result in—"

"Evolution," I interrupt again.

The knowing ghost frowns. "I am quite capable of finishing my own sentences. Are you sure your judgement hasn't become clouded by sentimentality? Of all the thousands of tribes beyond these walls, how can you be certain this one, which you've only known a short time, is deserving of your intercession? Your actions might eventually undo all that Jod has done to restore this planet. Perhaps, in the natural order of things, it is simply their time to perish from the Earth."

"Is my device's remote audio receptor still slaved to your headpiece?"

The lines on his brow arc quizzically. "It is."

"Then please listen to it now?"

The appliance atop the knowing ghost's head illumes. By turns his face appears confused and contemplative, then finally...something else. He strides slowly to the corridor wall, unhinges his index finger to reveal an audio jack, and plugs it into a socket. The hallway fills with the sound of Tyro playing his trumpet—a piece I've heard him practice many times before, though I can't recall him ever playing it quite so well. The reactions on the faces in the corridor parallel those of the knowing ghost from a moment ago. The long line of Evols listen with rapt attention.

When Tyro stops playing, the knowing ghost removes his finger from the socket. "Our friend has come to ask that the tribe this musical Devol represents be allowed to live here in the citadel after our departure. I'm of the opinion that this planet, and all that's upon it, is the birthright of the Devols, and they can do with it as they wish, though I admit turning over this facility to them seems analogous to giving a child technology it cannot possibly hope to understand, so I leave the decision to all of you. Do you believe these Devols should now enjoy the protection of the walls that have kept us safe for so many years?"

One Evol nods, then another and another, until all the Evols standing in the corridor begin nodding in unison.

The knowing ghost turns to me. "You've imbued our parting with a bittersweetness, revealing among us a fondness for this planet that will never again be our home, most likely the last emotion any of us will ever feel, assuredly the last one we'll experience together. It'll be several hours yet until all of us are installed within our vessels. We've scheduled the transports to launch simultaneously at midnight, our final collective act. I'll arrange it so the moment the rocket engines fire the doors to the citadel's main entrance will open automatically."

My hologram bows in gratitude. "Thank you...and I hope you find on your journey that which you seek."

The knowing ghost grins. "I wish you the same, my friend."

Chapter Eleven

At sundown Tyro and I crest the ridge of the river valley that encompasses Canine Island. "The cooking fires burn brightly tonight," I observe.

Tyro slows and listens intently to the sound traveling across the water—the faint, but unmistakable, hue and cry caused by chaos and carnage. Tyro sets off at a run. I roll as quickly as I can to keep pace, but he's across the river before I've even made it to the bank. I lose track of him in the smoke engulfing the island.

I drop my projection and deploy my limbs to ford the river underwater. The first thing I see when I emerge on the opposite bank is Mongrel impaled through the chest with a spear. The dense smoke renders most of my sensors useless. I follow a trail of the dying and the dead to the heart of the camp. Atop the hill, I find Tyro standing over a slain opponent.

I raise my projection as I climb the hill. "Did you know him?"

Tyro turns toward me. "He was my half-brother."

"The chieftain of your former tribe?"

"Yes, he'd been searching for me during the melee."

I take note of the corpse's many stab wounds and the bloody tip of Tyro's spear. "By the look of him, I imagine he regrets finding you."

"I should've been here to fight alongside my people."

"What they need now is a leader, not a warrior."

"They've scattered, Imrad. How do I lead people running in every direction?"

I point to his haversack. "Call to them. They will follow you. Lead your people to Highwalls where they'll be safe."

~ * ~

Tyro runs ahead of a few dozen of the islanders. Every kilometer or so, he stops, turns, and blows his trumpet as those that follow him run past. Then he races to resume his position at the front of the group so they can continue to follow his lead. As we make our way through the forest, other islanders join our ranks, though we're frequently beset by a small strike force of pursuers, and each skirmish inevitably results in casualties, dwindling our numbers once more.

We reach Highwalls just before midnight. I fear we may have traveled too fast, for the front gates are not yet open. Tyro, seeing the formidable gates closed, forms his people into a phalanx with himself at its head. He blows his trumpet long and loud. Other islanders emerge from the woodland surrounding the citadel and stand with us in the clearing before the entrance.

Then the war drums begin to sound, their beating growing louder as the drummers draw nearer. When they reach the edge of the woodland, the drumming drowns out the trumpet. Tyro lowers his horn and raises his spear.

Hostiles step out of the woods, and we're soon surrounded on all sides. Disciplined, they wait as more of their members continue to take position around us. Tyro and the others ready themselves for the imminent attack. All at once, the drums fall silent.

My seismic sensor registers the tremors before anyone feels the ground rumbling beneath us. Suddenly, the night sky erupts into fire followed by an explosion of such magnitude that it momentarily knocks my audio receptors offline.

The next sound I hear is a mass wailing. Everyone, the islanders and the hostiles, writhe on the ground, their hands held tight over their ears, their eyes watching in awe as the columns of rocket fire streak toward the stars. The gates of the citadel slowly begin to open. I nudge Tyro with one of my small limbs as my projection points to the entrance. He rousts the other islanders still spellbound by the pyrotechnics and leads them into the citadel. A few of the nearby hostiles notice our retreat through the gates, but I project myself to ten times my usual size to frighten them off. Once inside, I quickly interface with a control panel and close the gates behind us.

Chapter Twelve

I access the citadel's computer network and study some of the facility's more salient systems. I adjust the life support settings and disable the offensive weaponry, thinking plasma cannons capable of disintegrating an advancing tank division might be a bit beyond these spearmen's ken. As the others in the group hunker down into nooks and crannies near the entrance for some well-deserved rest, I take a few moments to upload my memory, for posterity's sake, into the citadel's mainframe, even recording a brief prologue to introduce my account so future readers will have an audio sample of my voice. It's been ages since I've done any storytelling.

"'Everything really got started on what I'd been led to believe was the second Tuesday of February.'"

Tyro leans in the doorway of the workstation. "What's a February?"

"How long have you been standing there?"

"For a while now. I think the evening's mayhem may've scrambled some of your workings, though the same could probably be said of us all. I was going to have a look around while the others slept. Thought maybe you could give me the tour since you're familiar with this place."

"Are you sure you're not too tired?" I ask.

"I don't think I'll be able to sleep for days."

"Once you finally do sleep, it'll likely be for days."

~ * ~

We enter the long greenhouse off the capacious atrium. Tyro takes in the lush environs. "I've never seen such fruit."

"According to the schematics I downloaded, there's an orangery up ahead."

"Orangery?"

My hologram can't help but smile. "A place for growing oranges."

"Is that another type of fruit?"

"I think you're going to like it here." I point to the small tubes that run through the foliage. "Those connect to the filtration system. No more drinking water that's been pissed in upriver."

He considers the rows of tomato plants and grapevines. "This is how I imagined the afterlife to be."

"It might seem like paradise at first, but soon the trouble will start."

"What trouble?"

"The inevitable kind rooted in human nature," I answer. "When there's a little, people fight over what little there is, but when there's a lot, people fight over even less, just to have a little more than their neighbor, despite having as much as they'll ever need. Since you haven't lived with abundance before, you haven't experienced that particular human failing. However, if the past can be relied upon as an indicator of the future, I'm afraid in time you will."

"So what can I do to prevent this trouble?"

"Nothing can prevent the inexorable, but you might be able to forestall it...for a while."

"How?"

"You've proven yourself the rightful chieftain of the people you led here tonight, but you could also be the leader to those out there. Tomorrow, visit your former tribe, mourn your brother's death, and invite those who would follow you to live within these walls and share in all this place has to offer...just like the day we met when you invited your erstwhile pursuers to share dogmeat. If you can grow a culture of taking less, of sharing, cultivate cooperation and weed out conflict, then you'll have created a garden far greater than this one."

Tyro walks slowly past the orange trees. "Now that my people are finally safe, you're instructing me to invite those who killed our fallen tribesmen to live here in Highwalls side-by-side with us and share in that which we've only just discovered?"

"I'm not instructing you to do anything. I'm less than air, whereas you're stone and sinew, so the decision is yours alone. I understand how the course of action I'm suggesting contradicts with the feelings you harbor for those who've wronged your people, but through all my years of living, I've come to learn having contradictory ideas in your head is a side effect of being human."

"I'll think on it."

"I know you will."

We exit the greenhouse, and I suggest we climb the many steps to the parapets surmounting the ramparts of Highwalls. At the top, Tyro peers over the side at the ground far below and the forest beyond as I study the enormity of the open area from which we've just ascended. From this vantage point, I realize Jodian's citadel had most likely once been a sports arena, repurposed and renovated over the centuries. I survey the lingering smoke issuing from the underground rocket silos that stipple the field around the atrium. Could this place have been the model for the stadium where I was separated from Rad?

"I've never been up this high before. Everything down there seems so small."

"It's called the Overview Effect."

"I almost feel as if I could touch the stars above us. It must be lonely up there."

"If only being human could cure loneliness."

Tyro turns to me. "I always see you so much better at nighttime. You've been like a brother to me, Imrad."

"That's what you've always wanted, isn't it? A brother who wouldn't betray you." I lower my gaze from the vault of the sky and look at the concrete floor then the steel wall of the parapet Tyro leans against. "As you're probably aware, the device that projects my image is what actually does the seeing, not the image itself. Would you mind picking me up and placing me on the wall next to you so I might see below as well as above?"

Tyro lifts me up and sets me atop the parapet near his shoulder. I take note of the rocky ground at the base of the rampart.

"What are you thinking about?" Tyro asks.

"The gravity of our situation."

"How do you mean?"

"The Evols who dwelled here chose to relinquish their agency when they decided to abandon this place, forfeiting their free will to move about these confines for predetermined trajectories through the vast emptiness of space. I have personal experience with that sort of existence and could never knowingly live that way again, but then this world truly is for the living, and the actual me died long ago."

"Imrad, your words are a mystery to me tonight."

"I don't mean for them to be...perhaps I just don't know the correct combination of words to clearly express my thoughts in this moment. My real brother once told me that part of being human is not always knowing what to say, so right now I'll simply say goodbye."

I watch Tyro's changing countenance as I fall to the rocks below.

About the Author

Wes Payton has a B.A. in English/Rhetoric/Philosophy and an M.A. in English. He has been a short-story presenter for the Illinois Philological Association. His play *Way Station* was selected for a Next Draft reading in 2015, and *What Does a Question Weigh?* was selected for a staged reading as part of the 2017 Chicago New Work Festival. He is the author of the novels *Lead Tears, Darkling Spinster, Darkling Spinster No More, Standing in Doorways, Raison Deidre, Intimate Recreation, Oblong, The House Painter and the Pirate Hunter, Downstate Illinois, Immurdered: Some Time to Kill, Dissimiles: More's the Pity, Namastab: Transition into Decompose,* and *Jackassignation: Too Clever by Half.* Wes and his family live in Oak Park, Illinois. You can find out more about his work at: http://wespayton.weebly.com/